JESSICA WATKINS PRESENTS

MAKE IT TO ME

ELISABETH

"If you're going to love someone or something
Then don't be a leaking faucet- be a hurricane."

-Shannon L. Alder

PRESENT

Rich felt the tightness of the ropes embedded into his skin as he pulled on them. He hated that he was tied to a chair and that it wasn't going to be as easy getting out of them as he thought. He figured he had to distract her as he tried to ease both his pain and the ropes.

Rich looked around the room he was in; the room definitely gave him the creeps. It was a disgusting and dirty abandoned clinic. He caught sight of a rat running from one area to the next and shuddered at the thought of how many rats were all over the place. He truly hated rats.

The place reminded him of an episode of a television show that showed the abandoned places all over the world. He wouldn't have been surprised this place had been on there.

The windows were still intact. All Rich could see were trees, and he wondered how long he had been out in order to be somewhere he didn't recognize. He shut his eyes temporarily, trying to muster up all the rational thoughts he had left before setting this psycho off, putting not only him, but also his love at risk.

"Lydia? I get that something happened to you. I can see the look in your eyes, but that doesn't mean what you're doing is right," Rich said, trying to get through to her. But she switched up on her and shut the vulnerable one out.

"You know nothing about me, Rich Bautista," she said. "You think you know because of poor little Michael? He doesn't know me either. None of you do. If you did, then I wouldn't be alone in this world."

Lydia looked down.

"First of all, you weren't alone in this world," Rich angrily said. "You had Michael but he wasn't enough for you. You had your twin, whom you killed."

"*I did it for you! She was cheating on you!*" Lydia yelled in Rich's face. Before Rich could get another word out, she punched him repeatedly until his face was full of blood. Lydia stopped and was breathing loudly.

"She wasn't cheating on me," Rich said. "She was part of my team. She was a cop. You killed your innocent twin all because you were jealous of her. Don't use me as an excuse for your hatred, Lydia."

"You know nothing," Lydia snapped. "All you're trying to do is confuse me so that I'll let you go, but know that I'm not letting you go. You're dying here like the rest of them."

Rich looked at her with no emotion. "I didn't plan on letting you go either. If I'm dying here, so are you pretty lady."

He finished the sentence with a smirk.

"Shut up."

Lydia angrily stabbed a syringe into Rich's neck. . Rich screamed as the substance ran through his veins. He felt like his whole body was being torn apart, and he couldn't hold it in even if he tried. He screamed at the top of his lungs. Lydia started laughing—she loved that he screamed. It made her happy.

"I love that sound so much more than when you're talking," Lydia said.

Rich finally was able to breathe. His gray tee shirt was soaked in his sweat. *This isn't going to be how things end,* Rich thought to himself. He knew that his team would find him sooner or later due to the cell phone in his pocket. He knew that Lydia was in a rush because she didn't bother removing anything from him except for his gun.

Lydia dragged a chair in front of Rich and held his gun in her hands as she pointed it at him. "You took everything away from me, Rich. You know that! You took my sister from me, you're trying to take my precious Francesca from me, and you took my baby away from me. You know Reese isn't yours, she's mine!"

Rich shook his head from side to side. He knew she was unraveling and it pleased him. "She's not yours, Lydia. I never took anything from you. You took my friend, Melissa from the both of us. You chose to end her life because of selfish reasons. Don't blame me for being sick in the head, do you hear me?"

"I'm sick?" Lydia repeated.

Rich looked at her, filled with disgust. Then he felt a burn on his side as he realized that Lydia had shot him out of anger. He couldn't even reach for his side as he cried out in pain. He started to cough up blood, and wished he was free and able to end her right there, right now!

Rich finally stopped coughing and looked at her with eyes full of rage. "You're dying by my hands."

Lydia laughed as she shot him again in the same area. Rich screamed louder than he had ever screamed in his life. Then she stood up abruptly and injected him with the same substance, making him scream again. Tears streamed down his bloody face and she licked both the tears and blood, giving Rich goosebumps as he tried to move his face away from her tongue.

"You taste amazing," she said as she went back to sit in front of Rich. "Just as amazing as Francesca. If I didn't love her, I'd love you, but I chose her."

As Lydia had her back turned, Rich was able to get his legs loose. Lydia was close enough to him that he could smell the faint scent of her hair. It was a citrusy smell, which didn't match her character at all. Rich thought his plan over in his head, the fastest, efficient way to put her to sleep was reaching for her neck. He used all of his strength to lift himself up and used his legs to choke her. He refused to let go until he heard her voice straining, but he knew she wasn't dead so he waited until she was knocked unconscious. He tried his best to free himself using his teeth to get his wrists free . His teeth gripped the ropes harder causing them to loosen and unravel from the grip the had on his wrists. It took him almost a half hour to get out of everything. When he did, Lydia was waking up.

She tried to lunge at him and he leaped out of the chair. Lydia grabbed his leg and Rich fell onto his wounded side. He screamed out in pain but turned around to kick her in the face so she could let go of him. Rich looked at where his gun dropped when he was choking Lydia. He rushed over to get it, but she hit him on his shoulder with a hammer. Rich, running on adrenaline, didn't register the pain as he grabbed his gun, turned around, and emptied the rest of his bullets inside her.

Lydia dropped right onto him, bleeding out on him, coughing and laughing at the same time. Rich felt her heartbeat above him as it slowed until it didn't beat any longer. As Rich felt his own life slip away, he smiled at the fact that his girl and his daughter would be okay now. He wasn't sure if he was losing it or what, but he could've sworn after however long it was, he'd heard his people coming in.

By the time they found him, Rich was already unconscious.

CHAPTER 1
Five Months Ago

Fancy grabbed some herbal tea. It was time for her shift to be over at the hospital. She couldn't believe that she had graduated almost four years ago and was doing her last year of her psychiatry residency. At first, she'd dreaded working in triage as the psychiatrist, but she was so happy that she'd stuck with it because she loved it now. She had met all sorts of patients that she loved talking to about their lives, but she still dreaded one person who had made it his life's mission to be in her presence.

She took her tea and headed to do her last rounds and paperwork before she went home. *It would be great to go home on time for once*, she thought.

Just as she finished her paperwork and rounds, the paramedics came in rushing with two patients, and Fancy knew it was too good to be true that she would leave work on time. She put her tea down and went to go help since she was still the doctor on the floor.

One patient, a gunshot victim, had gone into surgery. The victim had been shot in the neck and was bleeding profusely. Fancy didn't have all the details, but she knew that this was more than a mistake.

The other patient was the driver who'd hit the gunshot wound victim's car as it spiraled out of control on the road. The second patient was okay, but had to be taken to x-ray to determine if anything was fractured or broken.

Once she was finished, she handed everything over to the next doctor on the floor.

Fancy looked up and saw the chief of surgery walking towards her, Michael Burns. He was such a fine man in her eyes. He had beautiful green eyes, and was six feet and fit, neither too muscular nor skinny. He was bi-racial, and had the most beautiful smile she'd ever seen in her life. Fancy was attracted to him, but she tried her best to hide it. She ran her fingers through her short hair that she never once grew long, and she loved it.

Fancy tried to act like a professional when he finally reached her.

"Hey, Dr. Imani. I mean, Fancy. Are you going home now?"

Fancy was fixated on the way his mouth moved. She knew she should've snatched herself out of this trance, but she couldn't help but be mesmerized by him.

After staring at his mouth a minute too long, Fancy cleared her throat and decided to finally speak. "Yes, sir. I am," she said with a smile.

Michael smiled back at her. "Oh okay. Well, I just got here. You need to get some sleep, and before you go, there are two detectives here who need to talk to you to get some information on your patients." He then pointed in the direction near the entrance of the hospital behind Fancy.

Fancy turned to look, but because she was so exhausted, even her glasses didn't help her see. "What? What two detectives?"

Michael directed her slightly more to the right. "The ones right over there, Ma'am. Funny how you can't see and you have your glasses on."

Fancy couldn't help but giggle a little, however it was more because of Michael touching her than it was anything else.

Fancy nodded her head in agreement with Michael. "Yeah, it's been a long shift."

"Okay, well, one of the detectives says he's your boyfriend. A Detective Bautista."

Fancy turned back and looked at Michael, she rolled her eyes, and smiled. Of course Rich would say something like that, but it wasn't true.

"Oh, did he now?" Fancy asked with a smile as Michael suspiciously watched her. "Well, excuse me, sir. I'll let you get to work now. Have a good shift."

Fancy walked away and towards Rich. She rolled her eyes when their eyes met. These were the times she dreaded. She hated seeing Rich. He reminded her of university and how close they had become despite the fact that he was her roommate's boyfriend.

Francesca Imani thought of when she first met Rich Bautista. He was such a beautiful man inside and out, and he was down to earth for a man so beautiful. She hadn't had any classes with him and had only seen him when he came to visit his girlfriend, Melissa Clark, who'd been her roommate.

Melissa was petite with voluptuous red hair. She was five-foot-six, and a joyous and very outgoing person. Fancy met Melissa when she moved from Canada's capital, Ottawa, all the way to Los Angeles, California for med school. They'd been roommates on campus for their first year, and in their second year, they moved into their very first apartment:

That year, when Fancy had come back from visiting her parents for the holidays, she walked in and there he was, walking out of the shower with his towel wrapped low around his waist. Rich Bautista was a six foot two lean male with defined abs. He had the v-cut that Fancy loved oh-so-much. Fancy had never really been into Hispanic men, but Rich had made her reconsider.

He was olive-skinned with dark hair that was almost black, which he wore swept back. His dark eyebrows, light green eyes, and trimmed facial hair were perfect. Fancy had wondered whether she was dreaming or not. There she'd been in gray, baggy sweats and a black tee with sneakers. She was glad that her short hair had been styled, cut into a bob and curled. She'd felt as though she looked dumb just staring at him with her red, square-

rimmed glasses while he looked back at her with his arms crossed over his chest, smirking.

Fancy had cleared her throat and decided to bring her luggage all the way in the apartment instead of just foolishly standing there.

"Do you need help with that?" he'd asked her.

Fancy had been a little shy. She smiled politely as she said, "Uhh...no, No, I'm okay."

Rich stood in place and smiled at her. "I'm Richard Bautista, but call me Rich. I'm Mel's boyfriend."

He took his time to stare at her from head to toe. To Rich, she was beautiful—one of the most beautiful women he'd ever seen.

"Oh, hi. I'm Fancy, her roommate. Nice to meet you. Well, I'll be out of your way." With that, Fancy had smiled and started to walk towards her room.

Rich didn't understand his need to continue to hear her voice, but he pressed to hear more. "Okay, well, nice to meet you too. What's your full name?"

Fancy turned back around to face him. "Francesca."

When Fancy told him her full name, he thought it was sexy how she tucked her loose hair in the back of her ear.

"I like that better. It suits you," he said to her.

She didn't look him in the eye as she smiled. She was nervous, and he knew it, so he allowed her to enter her room with no interruptions this time.

Then she'd found out that he'd actually been an undercover detective, and there was a Rich that he had been working on around them.

She'd hated how every time he came into the hospital, he'd had the nerve to announce that he was her boyfriend when they'd never dated a day in their lives.

His presence reminded her of her roommate and best friend, Melissa, who was killed by the guy he had been looking for. Although it had been five years since Melissa died, Fancy and Rich never talked about it. They'd comforted each other, but in the wrong way, and that mistake still haunted Fancy.

After Melissa's death, Fancy and Rich had become really close. They'd leaned on each other because they'd had no one else. They were the only two that understood how much it hurt to lose Melissa. They had both been in a bad place and made the decision to not deal with her death themselves.

It had happened during the anniversary of the third year of Melissa's death. Rich hadn't been doing so well, so Fancy had gone to check on him. One thing had led to another:

At the Police Fundraiser Gala, Fancy and Rich had gotten a little too drunk. When they both went back to Rich's loft, Rich went straight to the kitchen to grab some water. Fancy knew why she'd drank so much; someone had talked to her about her best friend, Melissa. It was too much for her, so she kept drinking and drinking until she felt numb. At that moment, she felt as though she needed to sit under some cold water, so she slipped out of her black dress as she walked towards the bathroom.

She loved Rich's bathtub. It was inviting her in, and she didn't immediately oblige. Fancy sat on the toilet, first admiring the huge bathtub.

She didn't realize how long she had been in there, but it must've been awhile. When she'd first started, she'd looked through the cupboards for the essentials and had found a lavender-scented liquid soap. Fancy had then squeezed it in the water-filled tub before getting in.

Elisabeth

She pressed play on the iPod that was sitting on the dock and, after fiddling with some songs, she settled for Jessie J's song, Nobody's Perfect. Fancy gave in to the temptation and soaked. As she sat in the tub, dread overcame her whole body. She pulled her knees to her chest and brought her forehead on her knees. Fancy couldn't help but start crying when the next song came blasting through some hidden speakers—Maxwell's This Woman's Work. Fancy was so hurt, destroyed, and broken, and she wasn't sure if she could ever feel whole again. It wasn't just about her best friend being gone, but she cried also for her own scarred body that kept a reminder there for her.

Back in the kitchen, Rich had heard the music come on but decided to leave Fancy be. Then he heard Maxwell's song play, and Rich stood up and walked over to the bathroom. He slightly opened the bathroom door and there Fancy was in his bathtub with her knees brought up to her chest, her arms wrapped around her legs, and her forehead resting on her knees. Rich started to walk away but he stopped dead in his tracks when heard a sob escape her mouth. Then, she started to cry a bit more. For some reason, it hurt his heart.

Rich suddenly had a pain in his chest that became worse as she cried louder. He wanted to move away, but his feet started moving in her direction.

Rich shed his clothes and got into the bathtub. Fancy didn't even bother looking up. Rich inched closer with the water moving around because of his weight. Rich finally stood up, picked her up and then sat back down with her back to his chest. Fancy tried to move away but Rich shushed her, pulling her back to him. Rich kissed both of her shoulders and laid his head on her shoulders. He didn't know how long they'd sat there, but he could feel the water getting colder. Rich didn't mind—he just wanted Fancy to know that he wasn't going to leave her alone. That he was there for her.

Rich heard her sniffle and couldn't take it. He wanted to kiss her sorrows away.

Rich kissed her neck, making her shudder and sending a signal straight down to her womanhood. It was such a small thing, but it meant so much more to her. She fought the feeling as her body started to betray her. He turned her around and Fancy couldn't look at him as she didn't want to be trapped in the eyes that haunted her dreams every night, wanting and needing only her. Rich put two fingers under her chin, bringing her head up so he could see those beautiful brown eyes. When she looked at Rich, he saw that she was in pain. It wasn't physical pain because with physical pain, it could heal and go away, but emotional pain took a person's whole being and it took someone else to help them through that. He knew exactly how he felt about this woman that stared back at him with such hurt that it hurt him. He wanted her to know that he would be there for her no matter what.

When Fancy looked at Rich, those tears she held in started flowing down her cheeks. Fancy made Rich want to consume that pain for her so that she couldn't feel it anymore. For Rich, he didn't know what took over him, but he kissed her. He kissed her softly, giving her a chance to pull away, but all Fancy did was wrap her arms around his neck. Rich grabbed her by the waist pulling her onto his lap. Hozier's song, From Eden, was playing and she started to grind on Rich. Rich's body came alive.

Groaning, he sprung up as she danced on him with her delicious body. Rich's hand started to explore her body. Fancy didn't wait as she stood up a bit then grabbed him and let it slide inside of her. She threw her head back as every inch of Rich filled her. He fit perfectly as if he was made just for her. The thought scared Fancy, but she tried not to let it dwell as she fought for control. She needed to be in control at this moment, a moment she didn't want to let go of. A moment too good to be true and yet it was.

To Rich, Fancy felt so good, she fit him perfectly. She was the one made for him and he had no problem trying to let her know, showing her that she was the one for him. Even if they had both been drinking, Rich had never felt more sober or clearheaded than that very moment. He let her take want she needed from him because to him, he was hers.

Rich placed his hand on the back of her neck, leading her head back to look at him. They looked into each other's eyes, both falling into a rhythmic motion as their bodies connected. Fancy was close, but what drove her all the way was the intense look in Rich's eyes.

For Rich, it felt amazing, she felt amazing. He tried letting her take control a bit longer but he couldn't. He wasn't good at that.

Rich's hips started to pump into her. He was thrusting into her and her screams became louder. He smiled because she was a loud one and he liked them loud. He wanted her to say his name and forget all about her worries, but he didn't want to scare her.

He looked at Fancy, her tears stopped flowing, and her sobs of sorrow turned into sobs of pure ecstasy. Rich loved the way her nails were scratching his shoulders and when she bit his shoulder, Rich started to thrust even faster and harder. Rich laughed a little when her breasts were bouncing up and down in his face. He captured one in his mouth and Fancy grabbed his hair. Rich loved how

Fancy grabbed his hair and pulled, She couldn't stop getting louder and Rich loved it. He knew that if he could, he'd make sure the world heard how he made her feel.

Rich looked at Fancy again. He didn't want her to release without him so he slowed down and started to kiss her, their tongues intertwined.

"Look at me Fancy...Francesca. Baby, please," Rich said to her.

Fancy finally opened up her eyes and looked at Rich. To him, she was so beautiful and he just had to kiss her again.

"Let go with me," Rich told her.

She let go with a loud cry as he let go right after her with a loud groan.

She saw the love in his eyes that she fought so hard to believe. When she had her release, it rocked her to her core. She screamed Rich's name as she tightly gripped his shoulders, throwing her head back, unable to stop herself from shaking uncontrollably as she saw stars.

"Rich! Oh God, Rich!" she screamed. Fancy felt like she wouldn't stop shaking and she tried to calm down as Rich kissed her neck.

Rich wasn't done with her. He wanted her beneath him and he knew that would have to wait. He let her have the control she fought for, and ever in his life had he let any woman take control, but she needed it

With that one night of mistake, they'd become tethered together with a baby girl, Reese Francesca Bautista. She was the light of both of their lives and it brought them closer together than before. They weren't together, but had decided to co-parent because their baby girl needed both of them in her life even if the parents weren't together as they should've been.

Rich smiled brightly at her. Till this day, Rich knew Fancy had no idea how much she affected him. If it hadn't been for the incident, she would've been his already.

What was he saying?

Hell, she was already his and no one else would have her.

"Oh, hello Francesca," Rich said.

Fancy rolled her eyes even though she loved the way Rich said her full name. "Detective Bautista."

Rich loved how Fancy pretended as though she wasn't interested when it was easy to tell that she clearly wanted him as much as he wanted her. The way she was studying him made him feel proud. He looked back to where she had been standing with the other doctor and saw the way he was staring at them. Rich decided to be a little extra by kissing Fancy on the forehead. He looked down at Fancy who still had her eyes shut, and he loved how comfortable they were with each other even though they weren't together. His Partner Royce just had to ruin the moment by clearing his throat.

Rich laughed softly. "You remember my partner, Royce?"

Fancy sarcastically said, "Of course, Detective Royce. So how've you been? How are Macy and the kids?"

Royce smiled. "Oh, they're wonderful, Fancy. Thanks for asking and she misses you."

Fancy smiled back and continued on, "Oh, I'll join her for yoga tomorrow. These overnight shifts have been killing me."

Royce chuckled. "Don't worry, you look fine."

"Hey, don't hit on my girl," Rich playfully said to his partner.

"Rich, I am not your girl and can you stop telling that false information to people I work with?"

"You never deny it," Rich said as a matter of fact.

"Nor do I acknowledge it. Now, what can I do for you boys?"

Royce watched the banter between Fancy and Rich go on. This was nothing new for him. He loved how two people could flirt so much and still claim they didn't like each other. They already shared the most precious thing in this world. He didn't understand how that hadn't brought them closer together.

He shook his head as he and Rich finally decided to tell Fancy why they were there.

After what seemed like half an hour of briefing the detectives, Fancy got into her car and laid her head against her steering wheel. She hated seeing Rich so much because ever since that first time she laid eyes on him, she had been in love, and fighting the love that she had for him made it even worse. She loved every inch of Rich and she would be eternally grateful for the blessing he created with her, her daughter, but every time she saw him, she saw Melissa. It was hard on her because she had found Melissa's body on her bed, lifeless, strangled, with the name slut carved into her chest. Fancy cried—hard. She would never erase that picture from her mind and every night, she had more and more nightmares.

Fancy got home to her apartment, glad that she had found this apartment after the tragedy of losing Melissa. They'd never found the guy that had been busy killing the girls five years ago, and everything seemed to die down, so she felt kind of okay.

Fancy discarded her green scrubs, and went into the bathroom to wash her face and brush her teeth. She walked into her bedroom, faced her vanity, and sat down on the chair. Then she looked up at the mirror and screamed. She was so terrified, she ran out of her room, found her cellphone, and called Rich in a heartbeat.

"Aren't you supposed to be sleeping sweetie?" Rich playfully said as he answered her call.

"Rich..."

Rich heard Fancy crying and his heart dropped. He got up from his desk and ran to his car. It was the longest fifteen minutes of his life, and when he got to Fancy's apartment, she was outside in her bra and panties, crying.

"Francesca? Francesca? What happened?" Rich asked her with a panic filled voice.

Fancy saw Rich and she hugged him hard. He picked her up and she wrapped her legs around him. Although Rich had dreamt of this moment, he knew it wasn't supposed to be like this.

He walked into the apartment first and everything seemed to be in place. He continued on to the kitchen and nothing was a problem there. Then when he finally hit the bedroom, still holding her, he saw on the wall straight ahead in big, bold dripping red paint: *"You broke my heart! You're next!"*

Both Rich and Fancy recognized the writing and it was terrifying to see this happening again. It brought both of them back to the last months when Melissa was alive, and she kept getting threatening letters and e-mails. And it also brought them back to the day she died.

Rich pulled his phone out, called 911, and told them to get a unit out there. Fancy was still in shock, but she was able to get dressed before the rest of the team got there. She wanted to hide the big scar on her stomach that she'd gotten from the night that Melissa died.

Rich pulled Fancy to the side and he saw scared she looked, how fragile she was, and he couldn't let this happen all over again. Not to someone he loved so dearly. So he made a decision that he thought was best for both him and her.

"You're moving in with me, go pack your bags," he said without missing a beat.

Fancy looked up at him, curious to see if he was joking, and she saw that he was not. "No, Rich. I'll be fine. I'll just go check into a hotel or something."

Fancy understood where Rich was coming from, but she didn't want to overstep her boundaries. She didn't want to make him feel uncomfortable by moving in with him while this whole thing was going on.

"Nope, not gonna happen. Go pack a bag and please, Francesca, don't argue with me on this. Look what happened here. Just look! Now imagine if Reese was here with you. What the hell would've happened? You're both moving in with me. That's it."

Rich turned Fancy around to look at her bedroom. People were everywhere getting evidence and taking pictures of the writing on the wall. She nodded, walking over to her closet to pack her bags just as Rich said.

Chapter 2

Rich worried about Fancy throughout his entire shift. When he was finally off work, he picked Reese up from his parents' house. When he and Reese reached his house, she was already asleep in her car seat. Rich looked at his precious little angel through the rearview mirror. She was the best thing that ever happened to him. He changed because of her. She made everything dark turn into light. When she was first born, he knew he was in love from her crying, to the moment she held his finger so tight in her tiny little hands. Reese was a combination of him and Fancy. She had a cocoa skin tone, and a head full of curly, black hair. What he loved the most was that she had one hazel colored eye and one light-brown colored eye. Her smile meant the world to him, so with the threat that

Fancy just received, neither of them would be out of his sight until he found who was doing this!

Rich got out of his car and got Reese out of the car too. He loved that she knew her daddy's arms because she smiled in her sleep. Rich was glad that Fancy was off tonight or else he would've told her to stay home. Rich shook his head he couldn't believe he was calling it home for the three of them when they all didn't live there together.

He walked into his loft, threw his bag down, and turned his alarm on again. Rich walked straight to the bed where Fancy was passed out cold and put Reese down too. He watched as Reese cuddled with her mother, they both looked peaceful as they slept. . After he was satisfied with looking at them, he walked to his fridge in the kitchen to get some water. He sat down on the stool in his kitchen and looked out at his loft.

He loved the open space that he was offered. It gave Reese more running space and she was able to drive around her little Barbie car without bumping into everything. Rich loved the way he was able to redo everything in his house.

Straight ahead, the sink was isolated and the oven sat facing it, connected to countertops. The fridge sat next to the oven, and then there was a wooden, kitchen table with four chairs that helped make the kitchen look alive. Further down, there was the living room, filled with Reese's toys, and a TV hanging on the wall.

He loved his big, arched windows that gave him sunlight all the time. He looked up and there was his favorite part of the loft; the skylights that he put in. The first one was right over his head and the second one was over the couches in the living room. On his left was his king-sized bed where he saw Fancy and Reese peacefully sleeping. Across from the bed was the bathroom—luckily that had a door and was a room of its own.

He walked over to the bathroom to shower. Afterward, he passed out himself.

"You know I love you right, Rich?"

"Yeah I know, Mel, but why are you saying it like that?"

"You know why. This isn't going to work. You love her and I see the way you look at her. You've never once looked at any girl like that."

"What? If you're worried about me doing my job and playing my part, don't worry, I can do it."

"No, that's not what I'm saying. I know you, we've been friends for a long time and that's why I'm telling you that you should pursue something. Don't pass up this opportunity when the woman you love is right there in front of you."

Just then Melissa's dead body appeared.

"It was your fault, Rich. You left me alone. I had no one, no one but you and you knew that but you left me."

He saw her body, all the color drained. Her wrists were cut, the word "slut" carved into her chest, and her beautiful green eyes looked lifeless. She had on that pretty blue dress he'd loved on her, and tears were forming in her eyes. Someone then came behind her with a belt and choked her.

There was nothing she could do and neither could Rich. Then he saw the person walk off into Fancy's room and watched her sleeping. He touched her beautiful chocolate skin, ran his fingers through her short hair, and then he turned and looked through the vanity mirror and saw his own reflection, the image of himself smiling at him mouthing the words, "She's mine."

The person then turned back around and got on top of Fancy. He started to choke her, and he saw himself choking her. He saw her beautiful brown eyes looking up at him and she touched his hands to get him to stop but he couldn't, he wouldn't. The more she struggled, the tighter the grip became.

"Rich, Rich, please stop."

Rich saw her crying asking, begging him to stop.

"Rich, Rich."

Something snapped Rich out of his nightmare. He looked down and saw that he was choking the life out of Fancy and she was in fact crying, pleading, asking him to stop and wake up.

"Rich, please wake up. Stop, you're dreaming. It's a dream. Please, Rich please."

Rich jumped out of bed, stumbling on the sheets. He was horrified. He hadn't had a nightmare in so long and today's events clearly brought him back to his nightmares again.

Rich sat on the floor, breathing heavily as Fancy remained on the bed, making sure Reese was still asleep. As she was rubbing Reese's back, she wondered what the hell just happened. They were like that for what seemed like an eternity, but had only been five minutes.

Rich decided to finally speak up. "Francesca, are you okay?"

Fancy unconsciously rubbed her neck. "Yeah, I think so."

Rich stood up but didn't move from where he was. He felt bad because the last thing he wanted to do was attack Fancy whether or not he was dreaming. "I'm so sorry. I didn't mean for that to happen. I'm so sorry."

Fancy just shook her head, nodding that she accepted his apology. "How long have you been having these nightmares?" she asked him, concerned because she hadn't known he was having nightmares.

He finally moved and sat at the edge of the bed with his back towards her. "Just once in a while. Today was definitely something else. I've never reacted like that. I usually just wake up right after."

Fancy moved closer to him and rubbed his back to soothe him. She didn't pay attention to what she was doing; she just knew her friend needed someone there for him. She was curious, so she asked, "Want to talk about it?"

Rich shook his head. He didn't enjoy talking about what had happened and how he'd failed as a detective himself. He hadn't been able to protect her as he'd wanted to. He blamed himself for her death.

"Not really, no. I'll go get some water." Rich stood up abruptly. He decided to change the subject because he didn't want to talk about Melissa or her death.

"Do you want some?" he asked.

Fancy sighed and ran her fingers through her ruffled hair. "Rich..."

Even as he stood, he still had his back to her. "I'm fine, Francesca."

He walked away from her.

"Rich..."

Fancy called out to him with worry in her voice. The way Fancy called him made him stop dead in his tracks. He turned around to look at her.

Rich knew that when Fancy called him that she was worried about something, but he really didn't want to talk to her about it. He couldn't talk about how he felt like it was his fault that Melissa was dead, and that this was happening to her. He just blamed himself for everything.

"Fancy..." Rich warned. He didn't feel like pressing on with this matter.

Fancy was going to keep talking, but she saw Reese waking up and this wasn't the time or the place to discuss this.

"Okay, okay, fine. But seriously, you need to see someone about that."

"Francesca, I'm fine," he tried to reassure her.

"Rich, please? If not for yourself, do it for Reese." She tried to plead with him. Even if they weren't together, Fancy wanted Rich to always be there for their daughter.

Rich sighed and agreed. He knew that Fancy knew he would do anything for his daughter. "Okay, fine, I'll see someone if they become worse okay? How's that?"

"Better." Fancy looked over at Reese who was still rubbing her sleepy eyes.

"Hi munchkin," she said with a big smile on her face.

"Mommy!!" As soon as Reese spoke, Fancy's worries went away.

Reese jumped up from where she was to give Fancy a big hug. Fancy kissed her good morning and smiled at her baby girl, whose hair was all over the place.

As Reese was hugging her mother, she saw her father smiling at her, waving.

"Hi Daddy!" She quickly got out of her mother's embrace and ran to her father. "Daddy, Daddy, Daddy!" She yelled as she ran to her father. Rich loved how energetic Reese was. She always woke up with a smile whether or not she was sick. She warmed his heart and made all his problems go away.

"Good morning, Princess," Rich said with smile on his face.

His baby girl, Reese, looked at him with the smile that melted his heart each and every time.

"Daddy, I hungy. I want ceweal. Pwease?" Reese asked with a huge smile on her face.

Rich just shook his head and smiled at his baby girl as he said, "Yes, lovely. Let's go get you that cereal."

Rich walked away with Reese in his arms leaving Fancy on the bed.

As Rich and Reese were busy talking to each other, Fancy reached for her cell to check it. As soon as she did that, she realized what time it was. She jumped out of bed so fast, surprised she held her balance. "Oh my! I slept until six in the morning? Oh, that sleeping pill knocked me out cold," Fancy said to Rich as he was in the kitchen feeding Reese.

Rich chuckled a bit. "Yeah, you didn't hear anything when I came in or when I put Reese down next to you last night?"

Fancy shook her head, "No, I didn't. I have to get ready for work."

"Same. You go ahead and shower first, Fancy," Rich said. "I'll get all of us something for breakfast. I'll drop you off at work then take Reese to daycare."

Fancy smiled as she got her essentials to go take a shower. "Okay, thanks."

***

*

It was a bit weird. There had never been a time where all three of them were in the same house getting ready to start their day. This reminded Fancy of when she and Melissa used to get ready to go out with the boys. The last time they had to get ready together was when they were all going out with Melissa, and all Rich kept doing was coming back in the bathroom to bother them. Fancy traveled down memory lane thinking about the good times back when she was attending med school and Melissa's roommate:

"Rich, Rich, babe you're bugging us. We're trying to get ready. Go watch television or something," Melissa said to Rich as she was trying to fix her makeup.

Rich laughed, "Okay Mel, I'll do as I'm told but first give me a kiss

Melissa gave Rich a quick peck and shooed him away. "Okay, better? Now go!" Melissa said as she tried to pretend to be annoyed at Rich.

Fancy tried her best to concentrate on her make-up. It was awkward for her, being around them when they got like that. She always felt like a third wheel. Where she felt like a third wheel, she had no idea that it was all an act.

She hadn't seen the signs pointing to where Rich and Melissa had been pretending to be a couple. For her, she just knew it was wrong to be attracted to her best friend's boyfriend.

As she finished her "barely there" makeup, she tried really hard to not turn around and look at Rich as he stared back at her in the mirror.

Fancy hurried out of the bathroom and went into her room to put her dress on. She looked herself over, glad she'd bought the black strapless mid-thigh dress. It hugged her curves right and it hid the little gut she had...well, to her she had it. Her large breasts looked like they were on the verge of spilling out before she adjusted them, and as she called them, her "birth-giving" hips and thighs looked nicely toned. She hated wearing heels, so she settled for her black flats. She knew she should've *been more feminine, but she just hated heels more than anything else.*

Fancy took the rollers out of her hair and ran her fingers through her hair, making the curls form more. She put on her pearl earrings. She loved piercings, so she had three holes in both ears and her septum pierced. Her motto was the more piercings, the better. She smiled thinking about how her dad had freaked out when she'd gotten her bellybutton pierced.

Fancy walked out and saw Rich opening the door for his friends, Tommy and Joe. She was relieved that she wouldn't be a third wheel again tonight.

Fancy walked over to front door where the boys were standing and said hello.

" Hey guys! Tommy, Joe, you guys clean up nice," Fancy complimented them.

"Thanks, Pretty lady," Joe said to her.

Tommy smiled at her. *"Fancy, I knew you'd notice."*

Fancy smiled at Tommy. He was definitely a looker. His tanned, olive skin was so beautiful, he had green eyes and long, blondish brown hair that he always had in a bun. He was the tallest out of everyone standing at six foot five, and then there was Joe who was about five foot eleven. He was the funny guy who she later found out was his partner, Joseph Royce. He was bi-racial with beautiful hazel eyes and always kept his hair cut short. He was a real charmer, but was always the sweetest one which was why he and Fancy always got along.

"So, Fancy, who are you are looking good for?" Joe asked her.

"Of course you, Joe. When are we going on that date again?" Fancy knew that she could harmlessly joke with him and he wouldn't think anything of it.

Joe couldn't help but laugh at Fancy. She was such a good woman inside and out, it made him wonder why she was still single.

"You want Macy to beat you and me up?" Joe asked as he winked at her.

Fancy shook her head. "Oh, I can take her. Don't you think so Tommy?" Fancy looked over at Tommy to see if he would've backed her up on what she was saying.

Tommy couldn't help but laugh. "Yeah right, you're a shrimp compared to her. Try fighting me," Tommy said as he flirted with Fancy. He winked at her as she shook her head at what he was saying.

"Tommy, tsk tsk tsk, now why would I go and do something like that?" Fancy rolled her eyes at what Tommy said.

Fancy walked over to the kitchen to get herself something to drink as everyone one else continued to talk. Tommy decided to follow her into the kitchen.

"Fancy, you know you want me," he said with a big grin on his face.

Fancy laughed and looked over at Tommy, "Tommy, you've got like a thousand girlfriends. Now why would I want you again?"

Tommy smirked, walking even closer to Fancy, "Because Baby, I can show you so many things, make you feel so many different ways you'll want to slap yourself for not doing it a long time ago."

As Tommy was saying this to Fancy, she couldn't help but get chills down her spine. Maybe it was the drinks she'd snuck when no one was looking. She had to stop looking at Tommy as he said this. She bit her lip as she looked at him from head to toe. When she looked back *up at his face, Tommy smiled even wider. Fancy cleared her throat and shook her head.*

Fancy looked away as she concentrated hard on the Jell-o shots in front of her. "You sound like a player. Now hush and bring the rest of the Jell-o shots in the living room." Fancy said, hoping that she sounded like she wasn't affected by anything concerning Tommy.

Tommy simply picked up the rest of the Jell-o shots off of the counter. "Oh baby, I love it when you boss me around," he said with a light chuckle.

Fancy couldn't help but laugh. It was true that Tommy was a man-whore, but what he didn't know was that if he truly stopped joking around and was serious for a second, she would consider going out with him.

As the night progressed, everyone was pretty buzzed as they climbed into the taxi van. Fancy sat in the front with the driver not paying attention to everyone else talking in the back. Then she got a text message and saw that it was from Rich, and all it said was, "You do look beautiful tonight."

When they got inside the club, they sat down in the booth as they all wanted to get a feel of the place. Melissa was starting to feel the buzz as she got Fancy and herself some drinks. Melissa and Fancy took a few shots then Melissa dragged Fancy to the dance floor. It didn't matter to either of them what song was playing, just as long as they were able to enjoy themselves.

Fancy got separated from Melissa but she didn't care. She started to dance with a random guy, but as she was dancing on him, she felt as though someone was watching her. Fancy stopped dancing, and turned around to see why she was getting that feeling. She looked around but didn't see anyone paying her any mind. Fancy shrugged it off as she decided to go back and take a seat in their booth.

As she sat back in their booth, she poured herself a glass of champagne. She looked up to where Melissa was dancing with some random guy. He was definitely a looker. Then she looked over at Tommy, who was busy sticking his tongue down some girl's throat. Fancy shook her head and thought, "typical of Tommy." Then she looked at the bar where Joe and Rich were talking to the bartender. They seemed to know him from the way the bartender was smiling with them. She looked back at Melissa who was basically dry humping the guy she was dancing with from before. Fancy shook her head because she applauded Rich for not being jealous or batting an eyelash. Fancy thought about it, and she didn't particularly want a man that was super jealous but she wanted someone who gave a damn.

Thoughts of Rich filled her mind and she tried to control them, but the alcohol filled her from head to toe. Just then, as though Fancy had beckoned him, Rich turned around to face her. The way Rich looked at Fancy, chills instantly ran down her spine. Fancy wasn't sure if it was the drinks in her system or pure lust. She tried to look away but she couldn't—there was something about Rich that kept drawing her in even when she tried to fight it.

She inhaled and exhaled as he stared at her. Whatever Joe was saying to him, Rich didn't hear any of it. It was as if everyone and everything was gone and they were the only ones there. Rich saw that some guy was walking up to Fancy, so he started advancing towards her without thinking of anything else. Before he could even take more than two steps, Joe stepped in front of him. Rich looked down at Joe's hand on his chest holding him back *from going to Fancy. Joe shook his head, which pissed Rich off but he understood.*

When he was calm enough to look up, Fancy was having a conversation with the guy and smiling. Rich tried to shake it off; he knew he had no right to feel jealous but he couldn't help it. Rihanna's song "S&M" started blaring through the speakers and Rich saw how fast Fancy stood up, grabbed the guy by the hand and led him to the dance floor. Rich followed their every move as they got to the dance floor and Fancy started to slowly move her body to the beat. He watched as she was facing the guy, which gave him access to her shapely butt. He became mesmerized with every move that she made.

Fancy turned around, facing away from the guy. She had her eyes shut not realizing that Rich was intently watching her. Fancy opened her eyes, meeting Rich's eyes. She wasn't sure what that expression was but he didn't look too happy.

The guy pulled her even closer and started to kiss her neck. Fancy told the guy to stop. She looked back at Rich, and he looked like he was about to explode. She got that he was angry but she didn't understand why. She knew he was getting angrier by the big vein in his neck.

Fancy was going to dwell on it but the guy, whom she forgot about, started kissing her neck again. This time, Fancy turned around and told him to stop. She tried to walk away but he pulled her back. She tried to push him off but he seemed to get stronger. She shoved him again and he fell back. Fancy was confused by this and looked at her small hands, there was no way she was able to shove the man. He was at least six feet tall and had bulging muscles. Then someone pulled her in the direction of the back door, and Fancy yelled and tried to *get the person to let go. Fear coursed through her body as she was being pulled, but no one seemed to notice. She couldn't perfectly see who it was as the alcohol started to affect her vision. As they got outside, her heart started to beat rapidly. She tried to pull away, looking around planning on running, then a familiar voice spoke up.*

"Fancy! Stop pulling. I'm not going to hurt you," Rich said.

Fancy was shocked.

She finally stopped pulling on her wrist and looked up at him. Rich looked pissed off at her which she didn't understand. She should've been the pissed off one since he'd dragged her outside like a jealous boyfriend.

Fancy sighed, heavily annoyed. "What, Rich? Why did you drag me outside? What's wrong with you?" she asked.

Rich started to pace, pulling Fancy back and forth with him.

"Rich! You're hurting me. Let go," Fancy said a bit calmer.

Rich stopped pacing and looked at Fancy's wrist which he was holding onto a little too tightly. He let go of it as if it burned him to touch her. Rich ran his fingers through his hair as he inhaled the nightly air. He knew he shouldn't have dragged Fancy outside, but he couldn't help it. When the guy had started kissing up on Fancy, he lost it. Joe tried to talk him out of it again, but this time he threatened to punch Joe. He knew that he shouldn't have threatened his partner especially since they were undercover tonight, but he couldn't help it. Both Joe and Melissa knew how he felt about Fancy, but he knew he had to continue with the charade of being Melissa's boyfriend. Rich had stayed calm throughout the whole *night, but when the guy didn't get off of Fancy, in that moment, he didn't care if he blew his cover. There was no way he was going to let anyone touch up on Fancy as long as he was there.*

"Rich! Did you hear a word I just said?" Fancy asked him.

Rich turned and looked at Fancy, who was pissed. He tried not to admire her, but there she was, ticked off at him with her arms crossed and tapping her little foot. Rich smiled as she waited for his reply and he couldn't help but be turned on by how upset Fancy was getting. Fancy rolled her eyes as she realized Rich was in his own world.

"Listen Rich, I'm not your girlfriend that you can just drag outside to talk to. What's your problem?"

Rich moved closer to Fancy and looked down at her. He was towering over her but she didn't falter.

"*Do you want to be my girlfriend?*" *Rich didn't think he'd actually just spoken the first thing that came out of his mouth.*

Fancy faltered and looked down. Deep down inside she was screaming yes, and everything was going off from her rapid heartbeat to the goosebumps all over her body. She thought about being his girlfriend for a moment, biting her lip and thinking of all the things she'd let him do to her body. She thought about his lean body and how she would lick all over his body. At the mere thought of that, she was dripping already and he hadn't even touched her.

Fancy dared to look at Rich and regretted it the moment she did. He mirrored her eyes filled with the same lust and hunger. She almost let a moan escape her mouth when Rich tugged at her chin to release her bottom lip and traced the freshly bitten flesh. Fancy blamed the alcohol for her reacting so openly to his touch. She was frozen in place as she watched Rich lean in to kiss her. She knew this was going to happen and yet she did nothing to stop it. Rich first licked where his finger had just traced. Fancy couldn't believe she could get wetter than this. She felt her knees give in just a little bit. Rich tipped her chin up and kissed her neck, slowly kissing every part of her neck, feeling her heart rapidly beating on his lips. As a moan escaped Fancy's lips, Rich roughly groaned.

He didn't bother with anything else; all he wanted to do was taste her lips. Rich fulfilled his own wish, kissing Fancy unexpectedly and snaking his tongue in her mouth when she gasped. He guided her to the wall, and when Fancy's back touched the wall, she was hit with a cold sensation against a hot one that was burning her all the way down to her toes. Fancy kissed Rich back, living in the moment, forgetting that they were outside in the back of the club. She felt Rich's member spring to life on her belly and she wanted to rub up against it.

Rich groaned again and broke the kiss. Just then, reality hit her and made her wake up and realize what she was doing. Guilt ate up inside of her as she thought about whose boyfriend this was. He wasn't available and neither was she available to him. She wanted to cry because she had done something bad against her friend, yet she was ashamed at how much, and how badly she wanted Rich.

Rich stepped back away from her, giving her space. She was confused by this guy. His girlfriend was her roommate and best friend. How could he be confusing her like this?

"Rich, you have a girlfriend. Please stop. Don't do this to me." Fancy felt too open and vulnerable at this

very moment. She knew she looked weak because she looked down and refused to look up at him. She just knew if she went down this path with him, she would get hurt. She knew she should've run away, but she couldn't move.

Rich placed his forefinger under her chin as he guided her to look at him. He just stared into Fancy's eyes. Fancy felt like he could read her mind, like she was too exposed to him like that. She needed to calm her nerves, but at this moment she felt like she couldn't. They were there for what seemed like forever, and then Rich sighed. To Fancy, he seemed to be thinking deeply about his next decision.

Rich stared into her eyes. He loved this woman and yet he knew it wasn't the time or the place to let her know. It would only hurt her more than anyone else when she found out the truth about the people around her being undercover cops.

"You're right, Francesca," Rich said as he leaned in and kissed her forehead. Rich knew he didn't want to let Fancy go, but he also knew it was the right thing to do.

Fancy closed her eyes when Rich kissed her forehead. She was overwhelmed with emotions that she couldn't begin to understand. When Rich let her go, she quickly walked away, practically sprinting towards the street to hail a cab. Rich wanted to kick himself because he knew this shouldn't have happened, but it did, and there Fancy was, probably teary eyed in a cab.

As soon as it happened, he messaged both Melissa and Joe to let them know that he was following Fancy home. He got into a cab right behind her and made sure to follow until she arrived home. He watched from afar as she safely entered her apartment. Rich paid the cab driver and let him go as he sat outside of the apartment building, wondering what the hell he had just done.

****

Fancy snapped out of memory lane and rushed even faster to get ready for work. After she finished getting ready, Fancy got Reese ready too. They waited until Rich was done in the shower so that she could do Reese's hair. This wasn't a routine they were used to, but they made it work for today. Fancy couldn't help but stare at Rich as he was dressed in nothing but a towel that hugged his waist. Rich was too busy drying his hair with another towel to notice what Fancy was doing. Fancy didn't mean to stare, but that was where her eyes were going.

She started from his beautiful green eyes to his perfect looking lips. Then she traveled to his defined shoulders. He turned around to get something behind him and she bit her bottom lip. She loved Rich's back. She reminisced on the feeling of his muscles moving beneath her fingers when he was on top of her. Every movement he made, she felt on her fingers. It sent shivers throughout her body. Fancy refused to shut her eyes as she stared at Rich's back. It seemed as though he was entertaining her as he dried his hair with a towel, his muscles rippling with every movement he made. Fancy had to hold back from moaning out loud with her daughter there. Then Reese shrieked because Fancy pulled her hair too tight.

"Francesca? Earth to Francesca?" Rich snapped her out of her staring moment.

Fancy smiled. "Oh yeah? What's up?"

"You're hurting my child. You don't hear her?" he said to her smiling because she got caught checking him out.

Fancy laughed. She looked at Reese through the mirror. "I'm sorry baby, I didn't do that on purpose." She kissed her all over her face until Reese started laughing, then Fancy gave her one more kiss and let her go back to playing with her Barbie.

Rich kissed Reese on the cheek too and walked out of the bathroom to get dressed.

Fancy finished Reese's hair and brought her out to the kitchen. She wanted to get some breakfast or at least some coffee before she started work.

Ten minutes later, Rich walked out to the kitchen as he was clipping his badge to his belt. She had to admit, he looked good in his crisp, white dress shirt and a black tie tucked into black jeans with his leather jacket. Rich looked up at Fancy as she was looking at him. He smiled at her. These were the moments he loved—moments like this where they simply smiled at each other without having to say anything. She understood him and he understood her.

His cell phone went off and snapped him out of that blissful moment. He looked at it and there was a message from his partner. It was time for them to go.

"Let's go," he said as he picked up Reese's daycare stuff.

Fancy looked at Rich, puzzled. "What? I can drive myself, Rich."

Rich looked at Fancy as though something had hit her upside the head. She must've forgotten that she agreed they would go together. "I know you can, but I'll drive you and pick you up. That's that."

Fancy looked at Rich to see if he was really serious with what he was saying. "Rich, don't be like that, just let me drive myself today and then tomorrow, yes tomorrow, I'll let you drive me okay?" Fancy knew Rich would agree because they were both running late.

"Francesca, this once. That's it."

"Thanks, Reese's daddy."

"Soon enough, it'll be Francesca's husband."

Fancy just looked at Rich—she had nothing to say. She couldn't deny it because that was what she secretly wanted. Rich smiled as he picked up Reese, and he walked over to Fancy sitting on the stool. He let Reese kiss her on the cheek, then he kissed where his daughter kissed, and then they both walked to the door. Fancy was left with a big smile on her face.

Rich turned around to look over at Fancy and said, "You think because I'm letting you drive, you're going to leave after me? No. Get your stuff and I'll follow you until you get to work."

Fancy shook her head. She knew there was a catch when he said she could drive herself.

Elisabeth

She finished off her coffee and put the dishes in the sink. She got all her things for work and they finally left together.

Chapter 3

Rich got back home later that night and didn't see Fancy's car parked outside. At first, he didn't panic because he thought maybe she had to do a double at work. From the times he was at the hospital, she worked doubles a lot so he sent her a text just to see if she was okay, but by the time he got out of the shower and didn't get anything back, he started to get worried.

"Hello? Umm, this is Detective Bautista. Is Fra—Dr. Imani still at work? Wait. Say that again? She left at three? Okay, thanks. Bye."

Rich threw on whatever was close to him and hurried all the way to Fancy's apartment. He was glad about two things; one, his daughter was over at his parents' house and two, he didn't forget his gun or else this would've been a stupid idea.

When he finally reached her apartment, he saw that Fancy's door was open and he walked in slowly, calling out her name. He then saw that there were signs of a fight, everything in her apartment was trashed, and there was blood on the wall. He started to get terrified. He didn't want this to be happening.

He immediately called for backup. Then, he went into the hallway leading to Fancy's room and opened the door. She was beat up to a pulp.

He ran over to her, checked for a pulse, and then called for an ambulance. He looked at her, noticing that her clothes were ripped open. He became murderous; he swore to himself that if this man had raped her, he would kill him with his bare hands. Rich couldn't help it, he stood up and started pacing back and forth. Then he felt a hand on his leg.

"Rich...Rich—" Fancy strained to talk.

Rich looked over at Fancy and kneeled down to her. He caressed her face. "Shh Francesca. The ambulance is coming. Did you see him? Did he rape you?" He closed his eyes. If she answered yes, someone was going to die.

Just then Fancy said, "She..."

And with that, Fancy passed out.

****

When Fancy finally woke up, it was two days after, and she finally felt the pain of getting her behind handed to her.

Fancy moaned. Her body was paining her. She felt like a truck had hit her.

Rich jumped out of his seat and ran over to her bedside. "Oh my God! Francesca, are you okay?" He looked over her to make sure she didn't turn or anything.

Fancy briefly closed her eyes. The room was spinning. "Hello to you too, Rich," she said as she opened her eyes again.

Rich moved back from her. Fancy looked at his whole demeanor and she knew he was pissed. This side of Rich was the side that no one wanted or needed to see.

"Don't 'hello' me, Fancy! I told you we should've taken the same car and when you decided to go to the apartment, you could've sent me a damn text. Now look at you!"

Fancy couldn't say anything. She had nothing to say. When Rich got this mad, it was best to let him keep lashing out, but her head was ringing from all the yelling.

Fancy put her hand over her head. "Rich, stop yelling."

Although he was yelling, he said, "I'm not yelling. Like…look. Did you ever stop to think about what would happen to me and Reese if you died or something?" He said, his voice moving over her like a piece of cotton.

He walked back closer to the bed and looked at her. He wanted Fancy to see that her actions weren't thought out. She put herself in a lot of danger that no one could've saved her from. He didn't want to think about what would've happened if he hadn't called the hospital or gone to her apartment. He sighed loudly, closed his eyes as he pinched the bridge of his nose.

Fancy felt bad because she knew she shouldn't have done what she had done. It wasn't anyone else's fault but hers. She reached over as far as she could to touch Rich.

"I'm sorry, Rich. I wasn't thinking. I just wanted to get extra things then she came out of nowhere."

Rich opened his eyes and looked at Fancy. He was confused.

"Who came out of nowhere?" he asked her.

"This is going to sound weird, but she looked like Mel with blonde hair."

Fancy felt stupid for saying that out loud.

Rich was a bit dumbfounded. "But we buried Mel. We saw her with our own two eyes, Francesca. You sure it was her?"

Fancy covered her eyes with both hands. "I don't know. Maybe I'm crazy or I'm losing it."

Rich needed to do some research, so he changed the subject. There were some things that Fancy still didn't know about, so he had to go to the police station and figure it out. He pulled out his cellphone and texted his partner Royce to meet him at the hospital as soon as he could.

He looked over at Fancy and said, "You're on leave for the time being."

Fancy looked at Rich as if he was on drugs. "What? What do you mean, I'm on leave?"

Rich looked at her as he repeated. "You're on leave from work. I spoke to your boss."

Fancy looked at Rich. She doubted that he had that much authority.

"Don't question it, baby. It's only for a bit until you feel better. I know how much you love your job."

Fancy shook her head and sighed. "Seriously? Who are you, my dad?"

Rich smiled at her as he sat back down in the chair. "No. According to the hospital files, I'm your husband, Mrs. Bautista."

Fancy rolled her eyes. "Shut the hell up, stupid."

Rich laughed. "You don't believe me?"

Fancy didn't even want to indulge on this again so she simply answered, "I don't care to."

"I'm glad you're alive, though," Rich said as he put the joking to the side.

"Same here, Rich. Same here," Fancy said as she reflected on the fact that she wasn't dead.

Chapter 4

Fancy woke up a second time since her incident, and she'd never before been in so much pain. She opened her eyes to look around and see what was going on. Did she have a dream about Melissa, or was she on something? Maybe it was the drugs. She could've sworn she'd seen Melissa in her apartment when she was getting her clothes, but the girl didn't have Melissa's smile or hair color. This woman was a blonde.

Then a picture flashed in her head of the woman hovering over her with a sardonic smile. The woman touched Fancy's face, traced her eyebrows, the bridge of her nose, her lips. Fancy couldn't move. She struggled to get up but her body wasn't moving at all. She closed her eyes and opened them back up again.

The woman was still there and the pain was real.

The woman took a pair of scissors and tore Fancy's dress apart. She stared at Fancy's scar and smiled. She mouthed to her and told her she'd done that—her artwork, her masterpiece...

Then she caressed Fancy's breasts, tracing down to her scar that was a slash starting from the left side of her bellybutton going all the way to her back, stopping near her spine. Fancy shuddered, tears started flowing from her eyes, and the woman licked Fancy's tears.

She looked down at Fancy and was happy to see how battered Fancy looked. She was beat up badly, but for her, this was love. This was how she showed appreciation. This was how she honored her most precious Fancy.

She slashed Fancy again, making sure that the scar now was complete. The slash extended from the right side of her bellybutton meeting towards her spine. Fancy was in pain, but she couldn't find her voice. She cried tears with no sound. The pain wasn't. She didn't know what this woman had injected her with, but she was paralyzed.

The woman repositioned herself again, put the scissors down, took a piece of cloth out of her pocket, and wiped some of Fancy's blood, sniffing it when she was done. As she picked up the pair of scissors and was getting ready to make another slash, Fancy found her voice and started screaming. Screaming like she was in pain. The woman panicked, worried that someone would hear Fancy's screams, and she ran, leaving her there.

"Francesca! Francesca! Wake up! You're dreaming." Rich shook her so she could wake up.

Fancy woke up with sweat all over her face and tears running down her cheeks. "Huh? Huh? What? Rich?"

Fancy looked up at Rich's worried face and she started to cry. She cried because she was happy it was just a dream and that she wasn't in her apartment again. She didn't want to relive the moment ever again.

It was the third time that month that Fancy had had that dream. It had been a month since she was discharged from the hospital, Rich never let her leave his sight. He was determined to keep her safe, so he took some of his personal money and hired a bodyguard while Fancy was at work.

Fancy had finally been able to go back to work the first month of being discharged and on bed rest. . During that month, Rich explained to her that he was working on something with the FBI and their police station to figure out who the hell the girl was. Rich and Fancy agreed to let Reese go back to Canada with Fancy's parents, who had come to see her. Both of them agreed that it was the best decision because the main person that needed to be kept safe was their daughter. This woman was targeting

Fancy, so they had to eliminate any possibilities of her kidnapping or killing their daughter.

Fancy was glad that Rich had been there for her, but she had to do something about sleeping in the same bed as Rich because she was getting used to it, and that was definitely not good for her. Of course, she was still fragile so Rich respected her, but what she didn't know was how hard it was for him every night.

He wanted to let her know someone loved her, he loved her, and he would protect her. He wanted to make her forget everything that happened to her. To replace every evil twisted thing that girl did to her to sweet beautiful serene memories. But he knew that she wouldn't accept him right now. Ever since what had happened, she'd worn a big shirt and pajama pants to bed. She'd told him she didn't want him seeing her new scar, and she was afraid to look at it herself too. So he did what anybody would do; He enrolled her in Krav Maga self-**defense** so that she would be able to **protect** herself should someone try to attack her again He still picked her up for work and dropped her off. If he couldn't, then the bodyguard did it for him.

****

Rich joined Fancy for her Krav Maga class. He was just in time for them to partner up. He walked straight to Fancy and picked her as his partner. She looked at him with a confused expression. She was used to him popping up at times because she never knew when he would pop up.

As they started to practice on each other, Rich never went easy on her so she preferred her other partner, Philip. Philip went easy on her, but Rich was basically beating her up. She tried her best, though, and she was glad she was able to get him a few times. Each time, like tonight, she would go home sore and have to soak in the bathtub.

After what seemed like half an hour of brutal training with Rich, the trainer called out telling them that they were done.

"Okay guys, that's a wrap. Thanks for coming and see you all tomorrow," the trainer said.

Fancy basically collapsed on the mat. She was breathing so hard. "Oh, thank God." She smiled, although it hurt like hell. She loved how she felt after.

Rich stood over her and smiled. "What's wrong, Francesca? Can't take the heat?" He reached out, stretching his arm out to help her up.

Fancy rolled her eyes, held onto his hand as he helped her up. "Shut up, Rich. I'm always sore when you're here," she said as she unconsciously rubbed thighs that were burning.

"I can take care of that," Rich said as he lightly smacked on the same thigh she was just rubbing.

Fancy laughed as she walked away to get her bag from the back of the studio room. Rich followed right behind her.

"Yeah yeah, Rich," Fancy said as she passed him his gym bag.

"I'm serious," Rich said as he grabbed his bag from Fancy.

Fancy looked up at Rich to see if he was serious, and as soon as she looked, she regretted it. She tried to look away but she couldn't. He was staring at her to the point where she felt like he could see through her and deep in her soul.

She broke off the contact as soon as Lisette called Rich's name. Fancy rolled her eyes in disgust and walked off before Lisette reached up behind her. Rich watched as

Fancy walked off. He couldn't help but watch her walk to talk to other people in the studio. Rich stayed back to talk to Lisette, and Fancy knew she shouldn't have been jealous of her, but she couldn't help it. Every time Rich was there, Lisette would talk to him but when he wasn't there, Lisette never really talked to her.

She rolled her eyes when Rich laughed hard at whatever Lisette was saying. She didn't need to feel jealous after she got her butt handed to her by the same guy.

Fancy left the studio and walked out to the lobby to sit down. She started checking her phone for any messages. She called her mother so she could see how Reese was doing, but her mother was busy. Fancy was a bit sad; she knew her and Rich had made the right decision by letting their daughter leave with her parents, but she missed her daughter ridiculously.

All of a sudden, Fancy felt like someone was watching her. She looked around, but didn't see anyone. It started to freak her out, so she decided to go back into the studio and wait there. As soon as she was about to do that, Rich came out smiling with Lisette. Fancy knew that she was being extra by walking up to Rich and asking for the car keys, but at this point she didn't give a damn. Lisette was surprised that she'd come up to them, but Rich gave her the keys and just watched her walk away. He told Lisette he had to go and ran after Fancy.

"Pass me the keys, mademoiselle," he said as he reached up behind her.

Fancy stopped walking, turned around and said, "Here, and stop flirting with Lisette. Disgusting."

Rich laughed because Fancy threw his keys at him. "Are you jealous?"

Fancy rolled her eyes and got into the car as soon as he unlocked it without saying another word. Rich got into the car and took Fancy's hand in his. She tried pulling away, but he kept it there until she stopped fighting him. Her heart was beating so fast that she wasn't sure if he heard it, Fancy finally looked up at Rich to see what it was that he was doing at the moment. He gave her the most seductive smile she'd ever seen in her life, and she felt like she was going to melt on the spot. While he was looking at her, he kissed the back of her hand, lingering there for a bit, then he winked at her. Fancy didn't have a word to say. She just stared at him as he did it.

She finally snapped out of it and tried to snatch her hand away. She smiled as she said, "You play too much, Rich."

"Do I now?" Rich said as he kept smiling at her. He put her hand back down on her lap and leaned in close to her face. Fancy's eyes grew wider as she asked herself what the hell was going on. This man really knew how to mess with her emotions and she didn't like being toyed with.

Fancy tried to turn away, but he caught her by her chin and turned her head back to face him.

Rich just wanted to look at this woman. She was beautiful and his. Then he caught something from the corner of his eye. There was someone watching them from across the street.

"Francesca, do you see that person across the street?"

Fancy tried to turn and look but he turned her head back.

"Don't make it so noticeable, baby. Just move your eyes, not your head."

Fancy moved her eyes only and saw someone watching them, but she couldn't properly see who it was.

She started breathing heavily as the events from being attacked started playing in her head.

Rich saw that she was starting to breath heavy and he wanted, needed, her to calm down. "Look at me. Breathe in, breathe out. I'm here, okay?"

Fancy felt safer that Rich was there. "Okay," she said.

Rich leaned in, kissed Fancy's forehead, then sat back in the driver's seat. He looked over at Fancy to make sure she had her seatbelt on before he started driving away. Rich didn't take any chances to wait for the person watching him to make any moves. He turned his car on and sped out of the parking lot. He looked in his rearview mirror and saw that a black SUV was right behind him. He didn't want to assume that the SUV was following them until he was sure, so Rich decided to switch routes.

Instead of going back home, he went towards the police station. He knew he and Fancy would be safe there.

The police station was two blocks away from where they were and Rich didn't want to risk anything by going anywhere else. He looked over at Fancy. She was quiet, but he could tell she was nervous. He reached out and held her hand, giving it a light squeeze to reassure her that she was going to be okay. Rich took a left, the SUV took a left. He took a right and the SUV took a right. Rich made a U-turn and headed straight for the police station that was on his left. He stopped in front and the SUV drove by.

"Fancy, I need you to go inside the station, get to Royce, and tell him to call me. You are *not* to leave the station until I get back. You hear me?"

Fancy turned to face Rich, unsure if he was serious. She had work tonight and she couldn't afford to randomly call in. This pissed her off; she hated people messing around with her like that.

"Rich, I have work tonight. I need to go get my things from your house."

Without letting the conversation go on, Rich said," Fine, I'll go home, grab your work clothes and I'll come pick you up before work starts. How's that?"

Fancy sighed because she knew there was no winning this argument with Rich. Once he' made up his mind about something, it couldn't be changed even if you begged him.

"Alright, but be careful, Rich. I don't know who or what this person wants from us, but it's too much for you to handle yourself."

Fancy was genuinely worried about Rich's safety. Yes, he was a detective, but it didn't mean he wasn't a human being.

Rich looked at Fancy, and it warmed his heart that she cared about his safety, but he wasn't going to do anything ridiculous without some research and proof.

"I'll be okay. I'm not going to do anything to put us in harm's way, I promise."

Rich smiled at Fancy and tried to reassure her that he knew what he was doing. Fancy was convinced and got out of the car. Rich watched as she walked inside the police station, and he didn't leave until he got the call from Royce.

"Royce, we need to talk," Rich said.

Royce knew his partner was concerned about something due to the tone of his voice. "Rich, talk to me. What's going on?" Royce asked.

"Royce, I need you to help me off the record. I have to go to my little brother's workplace and have him search some things for me. There was a car following us. I think we're no longer as safe as we thought we were."

Rich was really starting to stress out because anything he did, nothing seemed to work out right. Rich impatiently waited until Royce stepped out and into his car. Royce looked at Rich and vice versa.

"Okay Rich, tell me what do you need me to do? You know I'm with you through everything," Royce said and meant every word.

Rich let a breath out and told him exactly what needed to be done.

Chapter 5

Fancy couldn't stop pacing in Royce's office. Royce had assigned someone else to watch her as he joined Rich after the phone call. They were gone for an hour now and she didn't know what to do. She understood that they had things to do like tracking down the killer and figuring out what to do, but she couldn't help but worry. Just as Fancy was about to sit down, she saw Royce coming upstairs, but she didn't see Rich. Fancy ran to Royce—she needed to know that Rich was okay and he hadn't gotten himself into any trouble.

"Royce, where is he? Is he okay?" Fancy tried to sound calm but she couldn't. Her nerves were all over the place. She couldn't bear losing Rich, no matter what.

Royce softly smiled at her. "He's fine, Fancy. He's downstairs waiting for you so he can drop you off at work."

Fancy physically relaxed. She walked back to Royce's office to grab her bag. She rushed by mumbling a goodbye to Royce.

Royce followed her downstairs to make sure she got in the car safely. When Fancy got in the car, she looked over at Rich who was waiting for her to get her seat belt on. She did the first thing that came to mind. She reached over and hugged Rich. She was so happy that he was okay and nothing seemed to be wrong with him. She wanted to come off as strong but with someone following them, she was worried and her nerves were on a high. Rich smiled, happy that she was there. When Fancy let go, she caressed Rich's cheek, looking him over. Although she relaxed when she saw him, he wasn't physically relaxed. She immediately knew something was wrong.

"Rich what is it?" she asked him as she looked into his eyes.

Rich put his hand over hers, took her hand in his, and kissed it. When Rich kissed Fancy's palm, she couldn't help but want to cry. She loved Rich so much and she didn't want anything to happen to them. Rich saw that Fancy was on the brink of tears so he reached out and caressed her face. To him, she was the most beautiful woman he had ever laid his eyes on, from the moment she'd walked into his life until now. He loved how Fancy didn't break eye contact with him as he leaned in closer to kiss her.

As they started kissing, they lost themselves in each other. This wasn't one of those rushed kissed; it was slow and sensual, bringing tears to Fancy's eyes. Fancy kissed

Rich as though it was their last day on earth. She wanted him to know that she wouldn't trade him for anyone else in the world. Just in case anything happened to them, they both kissed each other, making sure the way they kissed was cemented in their brain. When Rich broke off the kiss, Fancy felt empty. He smiled at her, which made her melt all over again. He gave her a quick peck and a kiss on the forehead.

Rich started to drive off in the direction of the hospital. As he was speaking, he looked straight ahead.

"Listen, I'm going to tell you some information, I just want you to listen. I'm saying sorry in advance that I didn't tell you, but you didn't need to know anything."

With, that he started to tell her what she needed to know.

"Okay, so Melissa, your roommate wasn't really my girlfriend. She was undercover too. Wait…before you

speak, she couldn't tell you. We had this case going on
for so long and we didn't think it would've gotten that out
of hand. We pretended to be a couple because that what
part of our assignment. I'm sorry that we didn't tell you,
but we couldn't, especially after Melissa died. We didn't
want to reveal who she was to the public because then the
killer would've figured it out. When you said the person
who attacked you looked like Melissa, I told Royce and
we looked into it. We are still looking into it. From what
we know, Mel was adopted and was an only child."

Fancy didn't even realize that they were in the
hospital parking lot. She was trying to absorb the
information that Rich was giving to her.. She wondered if
her friendship with Melissa was just a lie. Everything was
being questioned from the relationship between Rich and
Melissa, to Royce's. She didn't say a word because she

wanted to wrap this around her head. Melissa had been undercover just like Royce and Rich.

Rich continued on. "Listen Francesca, I understand that this is a lot to take in. I'm only telling you because I felt like you needed to know that much."

Fancy looked at Rich. "Why didn't you tell me before?" she asked.

Rich faced her as he said, "You didn't need to know."

"And who decided that?" she continued.

"I did." He replied.

Fancy started to get upset. "So you're telling me that you didn't want to tell me because you felt like it?" she asked as her voice got louder.

"No, that's not what I'm saying. I'm saying you didn't need to know, that's all," Rich said once again.

Fancy wasn't sure what was pissing her off more— whether it was his non-expressive face or that he kept repeating the same thing as though she should've understood.

"Rich, we have a child together. A child that is four goddamn years old and you felt like I didn't need to know this information? Do you know how I've felt about this whole thing?" Fancy gave Rich no time to answer. She was too angry to let him talk. "No! You don't. You decided that it was better for me to feel like I had slept with my best friend's ex and got pregnant by him while she was six feet under. She got murdered, Rich. Murdered!"

Fancy felt like all her bottled feelings on this topic were surfacing. She tried not to cry but she couldn't help it. She got her stuff and got out of the car. Rich felt her pain and didn't want to explain to her why he didn't tell her.

He shut off his engine, got out of his car, and ran up to her as she was walking towards the hospital entrance.

Rich grabbed Fancy by the elbow. "Francesca, wait."

Fancy turned around. "What Rich?" she asked.

Rich understood why she was mad. She'd deserved to know, but he'd made the decision not to tell her. This was still a case for the police so her knowing wouldn't have changed anything on the case.

"Listen Francesca, I'm sorry that I didn't tell you ahead of time. It was my decision not to tell you because I felt that you didn't need to know." Rich wiped away a tear that escaped Fancy's eye. "Everything I do, I do cautiously and with precision. Everything except for when it comes to you and Reese. Reese was a surprise for both of us. She brought us closer and now here we are. I know you think about how you and Mel were best friends. I was her ex so that meant off-limits, but I decided to tell you the truth now because you deserved to know you did nothing wrong. Mel and I were close but not that close. She was part of the undercover plan and she played her part well. I didn't expect to meet you and want you but that's what happened."

Rich looked at Fancy for any indication that she understood what he was saying.

Fancy shook her head She wanted to understand Rich, but she needed some time to think this through.

Rich saw from the corner of his eye that the bodyguard was waiting for Fancy at the entrance. He sighed, kissed Fancy on the forehead, and told her to go work. Fancy loved the feeling of Rich's lips on her skin no matter where it was. She nodded at what he said and said her goodbyes.

****

Throughout her whole shift, Fancy thought about what Rich had told her. Was Melissa that good that Fancy had never suspected her to also be an undercover cop? Her heart broke for Melissa because while doing her job, her life had been taken away. Even if this was work for Melissa, Fancy still considered her her best friend.

Fancy was spacing out instead of filling out her patient's chart so much so that she didn't hear Michael walk up behind her.

"Earth to Fancy?" he said.

Fancy felt like her soul jumped out of her body and returned. She turned around to face Michael. She tried to smile and pretend as though she didn't almost piss her pants.

"Oh, hi Michael. How's your shift going?" she asked.

He smiled. "Well, you know, it's going. I just started which means you'll be done soon."

"I thought you worked this morning?" she said.

"Yeah I did. I'm doing a double. They needed an extra doctor to step in tonight. Molly isn't feeling all that great so I'm going to lend a hand."

"Oh okay. Well I'm going to take my fifteen, then I'll do my rounds," Fancy said.

"Oh. Going to call your daughter?" Michael asked. "How is she? I heard she went on a mini vacation."

Fancy had this off feeling. She thought about whom she'd had a conversation with when it came to Reese going to her mother's. She didn't tell anyone at work, so how would Michael know about her daughter being away?

Michael interrupted her thoughts and chimed in. "Remember, my nephew goes to the same daycare as your daughter? When I was picking up my nephew, I heard from one of the teachers that little Reese wasn't going to be attending daycare," Michael said with a smile.

"Oh yeah, it must've slipped my mind," Fancy said. "I'll see you when it's time for the shift change meeting."

Fancy started to walk away but Michael followed her. "I'll walk with you to the café, he offered. "I'm going to grab some coffee,"

Fancy couldn't shake the feeling that she'd never told Michael about Reese or whatever daycare she went to.

When Fancy and Michael finally reached the café, she was so glad to have a bodyguard even though he stayed in the shadows. She never knew where he was but at the end of it all, Rich had told her that the bodyguard knew where she was at all times. She relaxed a little bit because she knew that he wouldn't let her or Rich down when it came to her being in trouble.

"Well Michael, I'll see you soon. I'm going to sit outside for a bit."

Before Michael could get a word in, Fancy walked off fast in the direction of the nearest exit. When she felt that cool breeze outside, she inhaled deeply and exhaled. She reached for her phone and saw a couple of texts from Rich. She smiled at how caring he was to check up on her despite the fact that she hadn't responded. She wanted to laugh at the last one he'd sent, telling her to put some distance between her and Michael because she already had a man. A man that was ready to let any other man know she wasn't available.

Fancy dialed Rich so she could hear his voice.

"Hello beautiful," he greeted.

Fancy smiled at the way he answered the phone. "Hey Rich, umm I need to talk to you," she said. She sighed because she wished it was about something else, something more peaceful and less hectic.

"What's up? What's on your mind?" he asked, a bit concerned.

"I was talking to Michael—Dr. Burns—and he mentioned something about Reese being on vacation," Fancy quickly said. "I hadn't told anyone I work with that she was away. He said something about his nephew being in the same daycare as her. I just don't remember that information."

This got Rich's attention. As Fancy was talking, Rich sat up at his desk so that he could search "Michael Burns" in the database. As the information was coming up, he started to ask Fancy questions.

"Okay, so we didn't tell him anything about Reese which means he found out from someone else. Have you ever felt unsafe around him?" Rich asked.

"To be honest, this is the first time I've felt uncomfortable around him," Fancy paced. "I don't know if it's because he brought Reese's name up or something, but I felt like you should know."

Rich sighed. "Fancy, stop pacing."

Fancy was a bit taken back. "How do you know I'm pacing?"

"Well, right now you're worried about everything and when you're worried you pace. Also I can hear your footsteps."

Fancy had nothing to say so she stayed silent. She understood that Rich was observant and he knew a lot about her. She still liked that even without being around her, he knew what her reactions were.

Rich didn't want Fancy to worry about this. He looked at the information from the database. At first he didn't notice anything, but then he saw that Michael had grown up in the same foster home as Melissa. He thought maybe it was just a coincidence, but he decided to look into it some more. Rich completely forgot that Fancy was still on the phone.

"Hello? Rich?" Fancy said.

"Oh, oh I'm sorry. I didn't mean to not listen to you. What did you say?" Rich asked, hoping Fancy would actually tell him this time.

"Oh, I was just saying that I have to go and don't forget to look into it," she said.

"I will, I promise. All right enjoy the rest of your shift. I'll pick you up after. I love you. Bye."

Rich didn't realize he'd told Fancy he loved her before he hung up. He was continuing the conversation with her as he read over Michael's file. Michael's file was easy to find because he had been arrested on petty charges when he was younger, but nothing too big.

Chapter 6

Fancy was still staring at her phone even after Rich hung up. : She and Rich knew they'd both felt some way about each other. She believed they strongly loved each other, but he'd just told her he loved her and hung up. He'd dropped a big bomb on her and she felt like she was on top of the world. She wasn't sure why he said it, but she was glad he did. She wanted to jump around and scream like a little girl, but she straightened her back and cleared her throat. She felt as though she was gliding on top of the world, and even though she tried not to smile, all she did was smile.

As she turned around to go back inside, she couldn't hide the smile on her face. Fancy walked back to the floor to do her rounds. She was trying to hide her smile as she checked on her patients. She spoke to her all her patients and kept the smile on even through the shift change meeting. The meeting was finally over, and she went inside to change out of her scrubs. Just then, her phone went off and a text from Rich popped up stating that he was outside. Fancy stepped out of the women's changing room, and as she turned the corner, she bumped into Michael. Fancy was shocked but she tried to calm herself down. She wasn't afraid because she knew that Rich was right outside and the bodyguard was close enough.

"Oh sorry, Michael," Fancy said.

Fancy looked at Michael. He looked distraught. He looked as though something was wrong. She didn't get it. Was he sick? she asked herself, but when Michael looked up at Fancy and made eye contact, Fancy saw what he had. He was carrying a gun that was pointed towards her.

"Look Fancy, I have to do this," he said.

Without realizing it, Fancy's body reacted first and she started to move back as Michael advanced towards her. She was getting terrified.

"What do you want?" Fancy asked, trying to come off as hard but her shaky voice said otherwise. Tears were beginning to form in her eyes. She questioned why Michael would want to kill her or point a gun at her? She tried to plead with him again.

"Michael, please don't do this." Her voice started to break. "I don't want to leave my daughter alone in this world. Please, Michael. Please."

Fancy couldn't help but cry. She was so terrified. She thought about Rich and their baby girl, her family back in Canada, and all her colleagues she would be leaving behind.

"You know what I want. Fancy, I'm sorry about this." As Michael said this, he pointed the gun at her head.

Fancy looked around but saw no one. She knew there were no cameras around here in the basement.

Michael continued talking, "Stop moving!"

Fancy jumped as Michael yelled at her to stop moving, and she did exactly as she was told.

"Fancy, I liked you," Michael continued. "I really did, but you have to understand that I love her. She's been with me for a long time. She protected me when no one else did and I owe her this much. All I have to do is pull the trigger. That's all."

Michael looked apologetic as he felt and Fancy didn't understand why.

Fancy was confused. She always thought that Michael was a decent guy. He was a looker but she never went past that. Right now, in this very moment, Michael was sounding like a lunatic and she was scared out of her mind. This was the same Michael that she had been working with for years, but now she felt like she didn't know him.

As Michael was about to pull the trigger, Fancy closed her eyes. As she had her eyes closed, the night that she and Rich made Reese flashed through her mind— when she first gave birth to Reese and how much she'd cried seeing her beautiful daughter. The smiles on her parents' and Rich's parents' faces when they all met their granddaughter. Most of all, she remembered the way Rich had held Reese as she'd cried in the delivery room, the love in his eyes as he cried and thanked Fancy for completing his world with Reese. As Fancy thought about all those memories and the most important people to her, she started sobbing. She couldn't help or control it; she would never get to kiss Rich or see his smile. She would never get to hold her baby girl or hear her calling her Mommy.

After what seemed like a little too long, Fancy opened her eyes. When she opened her eyes, she didn't see Michael. She looked down and saw a lifeless Michael on the ground, bleeding. Fancy panicked. She was about to turn him, but her bodyguard, whom she'd never seen so up close, pulled her away.

"No! Don't touch him," the bodyguard said. "Come with me."

The bodyguard pulled Fancy away. She didn't get what just happened, but she needed to know if Michael was dead.

"Is he? Is…is he? You know?" Fancy didn't want to say it out loud.

"No, he isn't. I didn't shoot him to kill him. I merely wounded him and knocked him out for a bit," he said.

Fancy was relieved that Michael wasn't dead. Even though he had been trying to kill her, deep down, she didn't want him to die.

"Where are we going?" Fancy asked. "Where are you taking me?"

She knew that they were exiting the building through the emergency exit, but she still wanted to know where she was going. The bodyguard didn't answer her. He just led her to the emergency exit and when they got outside, Rich's car was waiting for them.

The bodyguard opened the door for Fancy to sit in the back while he sat in the front, filling Rich in on everything.

"What is going on, Rich?" Fancy asked. "We just left a man there to die! Michael was bleeding!"

"Calm down, Fancy, Rich said. " I called one of the nurses there to give them a tip, and don't worry, they can't trace it. Second, I called Royce to update him. When Michael is out of surgery, we will question him. What did he say to you?"

He looked over at Fancy through the rearview mirror to reassure her that he was listening.

"He said that he had to do it," Fancy said. "I honestly don't know what's going on Rich. I'm, I'm just terrified at this point." Then she looked over at the passenger seat and saw who was sitting there. She wanted to know who got her out to safety.

"Thank you, sir for getting me out of there and saving me from whatever was going to happen," Fancy said. She was truly thankful to the person who sacrificed and saved her life like that. She couldn't picture leaving Reese in this world without her.

"I'm sorry sis-in-law," he replied. "I'm glad you're safe though. I want my brother to be able to still have you around for a long time."

Fancy was shocked when she heard him speak. It was weird to hear him speak. It took her a second to realize what he'd just called her.

"What? Sis-in-law?" Fancy asked curiously.

Rich chuckled a bit before he spoke. "Yeah Francesca, this is my little brother Mason. Sorry I didn't introduce you before but I didn't want him or you distracted."

Fancy looked at Rich as though she was going to kill him. He always made decisions without consulting her and it pissed her off. She looked over at Mason. He did look like Rich from the light green eyes to the black hair except Mason's hair was cut very low. Fancy tried not to stare at the resemblance between Rich and Mason but she couldn't help it.

"Francesca, stop staring at my little brother," Rich told her.

Fancy looked at Rich as if he was mental for saying that out loud, then she sat back in her seat. She was still astonished that they looked this much alike. She knew he had a brother that was away, but she didn't know he'd come back.

Rich started to explain to Fancy what they were going to be doing and that they wouldn't return to his loft.

"Listen Francesca, we are going to my parents' house." Rich told her. "Their security is better and I think it's best that you stay there for the couple of days that I'll be gone. Mason and I will be gone to check something and I need you to stay safe,"

Fancy looked at Rich as though he had grown a third eye. He looked at her in the rearview mirror and hoped she just complied instead of saying anything.

"You're not serious, Rich. You just want to move to your parents' home and put them in danger? You could've asked me if I was okay with putting them in danger," Fancy said.

Mason looked over at Rich and shook his head. "Rich, you didn't ask her? I told you to ask her before you moved her here," Mason said.

"Shut up, Mason," Rich said. He knew his brother wasn't helping the situation by that smirk he had on his face. He knew he should've asked her, but in the position that she was in, there was no time to ask.

"You do realize I'm right, Rich?" Fancy said.

Rich didn't answer as they pulled up to his parents' home. Every time Fancy came to the Bautista Residence, it still amazed her. The double gates opened up to a u-shaped driveway. As they pulled up to the front, there was security outside. She agreed with Rich that yes, this was definitely safer for her, but she refused to admit that to him. She hated that he was bossy, a little controlling, and seemed to make all the decisions for her. Not only that, but he was okay with putting his parents into the line of danger.

They all got out of the car and walked into the house. Mason said hello to his parents and Rich did as well. Fancy smiled at Rich's mom as she gave her a hug.

"Hi, Mrs. Bautista," Fancy said.

"Hi, sweetheart. I told you to call me Marie, Honey," Mrs. Bautista said.

Over the two years that Fancy had gotten to know Mrs. Bautista, they became close. She was like a second mother to her. Both Rich and Mason looked like their mother and got their height from their father. Their father, Benny Bautista, was at least six foot five while their mother stood at five foot six.

"Hi, Mr. Bautista," Fancy said with a smile.

"Fancy, I told you to call me Papa Bautista. In my head, you're already my daughter," he said as he looked at Rich.

Fancy had nothing to say. She just smiled as they walked into the sitting room. Rich pulled Fancy back.

"Sorry guys, I just need to talk with her for a bit," he said.

"Take your time, son," Rich's father said with a wink.

Rich rolled his eyes and walked away. His dad knew he was going to marry Fancy because he'd told his whole family that she was his wife, no matter what.

Rich held Fancy's hand as they went upstairs to his old room. When they entered, he smiled, reminiscing on his old bedroom, but he shook it off because he had to talk to Fancy.

"What's up, Rich?" Fancy asked him with a look of curiosity.

Rich held Fancy's hand as he looked at her. He just stared at her as she looked back at him with a confused expression. She wasn't sure what he was going to say or why he was acting like this.

Rich cleared his throat before he spoke. "Listen, Francesca, I feel like its time I talk to you. First, I know you heard when I said I loved you."

Rich smiled at Fancy's reaction. Fancy had tried to put it in the back of her mind because she wasn't sure if it had been out of habit

Rich continued, "I meant what I said and I'm not taking it back. I want you to know this just in case anything ever happens to me. Woman, I love you with every fiber of my being. When did it turn out like this? I don't know. I just found myself falling in love with you through everything. I don't believe in love at first sight but with you, I think that was what happened. The minute you walked into the apartment with your cute little face, those sweats, and that beautiful breath-taking smile, I fell in love. I know you love me so don't try and deny it either." Rich smiled.

With what Rich was saying, Fancy felt like she'd burst into a million pieces.

To hear Rich say that he loved her made her smile like a fool. She knew that she loved Rich a long time ago, but to hear him say it out loud made her want to do back flips and just kiss him senseless. But she had one thought, *how did he know she loved him?*

"How do you know that I love you, Rich?" Fancy asked, smiling at him.

Rich smiled back as he cupped her face, moving closer. "You told me you loved me two weeks ago in your sleep."

Fancy had nothing to say. She had unconsciously told Rich that she loved him and it didn't disturb her. It made her happy that she told him even if she hadn't been awake to do it. Before Fancy could get even a word out, Rich pushed her against the wall and kissed her senseless. Fancy felt it through her whole body from her head all the way to her toes. Just then, Fancy didn't care about anything else.

She put her arms around Rich's neck and as he stood up right, she stood on the tip of her toes. The kissing started to become intense as Rich's hands started to roaming all over her body. Rich's hands cupped her butt and he picked her up. Fancy wrapped her legs around Rich's waist as they continued kissing. Fancy ran her hands through Rich's hair and pulled him even closer. The way they were so close together, it was as if they were trying to morph into one. The kissing itself was so intense for Fancy that a tear fell from her eye. She thought about what her and Rich had been through, how they created a life, and how much everything changed the minute he said he loved her. This was something she never thought she would ever experience— loving someone with all your heart. Kissing them, feeling like you're losing yourself in them, but finding yourself in them at the same time.

Rich broke off the kiss and stared at Fancy. He looked at the woman that he loved, the woman that he would give his everything for, the one who gave him the most precious gift in life.

She opened her eyes to look back at him. "I love you, Francesca Imani. I love you more than anything else in this world, you hear me?"

Fancy smiled at Rich. She loved him just as much as he loved her. "I love you too, Rich Bautista," Fancy replied to him. "So yeah, I hear you."

"Good." Rich kissed her on the forehead. "Let's go downstairs and figure things out so we can bring our baby back home."

Rich put Fancy down and shook his head. He didn't care that his parents, or anyone else, were downstairs. He wanted to be with Fancy and it couldn't be any other time than now.

Rich scooped Fancy up in his arms and took her to the bed. He laid her on the bed and she knew what was coming. When he put her on the bed, he started by kissing her feet, then he trailed up and kissed every part of her body. Rich removed every piece of clothing that Fancy had on, kissing every part of her. Fancy thought that she was going to have a heart attack from the anticipation.

Rich hovered over Fancy and kissed her senseless. Fancy wasn't even sure what to do with herself at that moment. As they were on the bed, everything was slowed down. Rich took his time as he entered her, took his time to make her feel great, slowly kissing her neck, her chin, and the back of her ear all while caressing her thigh. Then Rich flipped her over and she was on all fours, and he planted his hand on her back, pushing her further down as she arched even more for him. He kissed each cheek then lightly slapped them both. Without giving Fancy a warning, she felt him inside of her, and it took Fancy a second to adjust to him, but she did. Fancy tried to wiggle to adjust, but he slapped her cheek and told her to stop moving. Fancy started to tense up because it was really becoming hard for her to adjust to him, and she felt like he was splitting her in half. Rich planted kisses on her back until he was at her neck and shoulders. This made Fancy relax before he started to move.

Rich whispered in her ear, telling her to let him take control, and for her to be his. Fancy wanted to tell him anything he wanted to hear, but with the way he was moving, Rich brought Francesca to the brink of tears. Happy tears. He made her see stars, and her eyes roll to the back of her head.

Chapter 7

The next day when Michael woke up, Rich and Royce were on their way to question him. He was still in handcuffs in a private hospital room. Michael tugged at his handcuffed wrists wincing at the pain. He looked out and saw that there were two police officers standing guard outside of his hospital room. He wanted to scream and run out but he couldn't do that at the moment. He looked around the room, it was like any other hospital room; his bed and the tacky bed sheets, an outdated television box set too far for his reach. He rolled his eyes when he realized that they removed everything else from the room, he had nothing. He inwardly groaned when he saw Rich and Royce walking in the room.

At first, Michael resisted. He refused to tell them who was behind the killings, and who was responsible for Melissa's death.

"Listen Michael, I understand that you care for her but don't you want to protect her from herself?" Rich asked him.

"Care for her?" Michael replied. "I don't just care for her, I love her and that's why I have nothing to say. She can protect herself. She would never harm herself."

Rich sighed and pinched the bridge of his nose. He knew that he could make a breakthrough with Michael; he just wasn't sure how long that would take. He needed to catch this person that was busy stalking and trying to kill the love of his life.

"Listen Michael, I understand that, but what I want to know is why?" Rich asked.

"Why what?" Michael asked, a confused expression written all over his face. He wasn't prepared when Rich asked him the next question.

"Why did she want you close to Francesca? Why did she kill Mel? Why Michael? Why?" Rich was growing impatient with Michael. He thought about how lucky Michael was that he didn't just punch him where he'd gotten shot. Rich shook his head and turned his back as Royce stared at Michael until he felt uncomfortable.

"Why are you looking at me like that?" Michael asked Royce.

Royce smiled. Everyone knew what kind of team he and Rich were. Rich was the cop that ultimately got everything out of the perp, but Royce contributed by making them uncomfortable. He stared at the perp until they either started to get irritated or annoyed. Either way, it worked because they always wanted to be away from

Royce. To them, he seemed like a weirdo and that gave them the creeps.

Royce looked over at Rich and then looked back at Michael. "Well Michael, I think my partner here just asked you a question, no?" Royce asked.

Michael rolled his eyes and tried to avoid Royce's stares and creepy smiles. "Honestly, you're giving me the creeps. Stop looking at me like that! What's your issue?"

Royce just looked at him and laughed. "Well, I can stop looking at you if you decide to answer my partner's questions. It's really that simple."

Michael shut his eyes and sighed. He was in pain even though they had given him pain medications. He started to get a headache just thinking about this whole situation. He knew why he decided to get involved. He loved her, yes, but he had to cut himself a deal before he wasn't offered one at all.

"I'll talk if I get a deal," Michael said, his eyes still shut.

Royce and Rich looked at each other. Then, Rich nodded.

"The D.A. can offer you ten years and maybe parole depending on how much information we get," Rich said, glad he'd had a talk with the DA before he got to the hospital or else this would've taken longer.

"Fine," Michael said. He sighed as he continued, "I need you to understand that I love her. She is the reason why I am where I am but I don't wish for her to be hurt. She means the world to me and that's why she needs to be caught. Lydia and Melissa are twins, but Mel didn't know of Lydia until about a year before she got killed. Melissa was easy to take advantage of because she had a soft spot for Lydia, and it was too late when she found out how much hate Lydia actually had for her. Lydia hated her because she got the life that she'd always wanted. Melissa was able to live with parents that loved her even though she wasn't their own. Lydia is a very manipulative person, but she has her reasons for being like that so please understand her like I do. After knowing so much about Melissa, Lydia became obsessed with everything in her life. She became obsessed with you and with Fancy."

Rich looked at Michael. He deserved to know the full story whether Michael wanted to tell it or not.

"Tell me what happened? Why did she kill Melissa?" Rich asked.

Michael looked to the wall. He saw the hurt in Rich's eyes and he didn't want to feel bad for Rich.

"She killed Melissa because she saw her meet up with a dude one night, and she thought Melissa was cheating on you. This was before we both found out you were a cop. Lydia killed Melissa and scarred Fancy because Fancy let it happen. She wanted to kill Melissa from the beginning and live her life, but she felt she needed to eliminate all the people that caused issues around Melissa and get new friends. As for Fancy, I was doing her a favor."

Rich decided not to show any facial expressions as Michael was explaining. He didn't want Michael to think he could stir up his emotions.

"What favor were you doing for her Michael?" Royce asked.

Michael looked at Rich as he said, "Lydia was becoming obsessed with Fancy. She was starting to love her. She loved everything Fancy did, from the way she smiled to how much care she showed to her patients. When I worked at the hospital, Lydia came sometimes. She hid very well so that Fancy couldn't see her. She wanted to admire her from afar, and she said Fancy's beauty was inside and out unlike anyone else she'd ever met. She fell more in love with Fancy when she had Reese."

Before Michael could continue, Rich moved in closer to Michael and said through clenched teeth, "Don't say my daughter's name out of your dirty mouth. Are we clear?"

Michael's heart started beating a bit faster. He saw the anger in Rich's eyes. He knew for sure that he didn't want to piss anyone off right now because he needed that deal to survive everything that was coming his way.

Michael nodded. "I understand," he said. Royce signaled him to continue talking.

Michael began again, "When Fancy had her baby, Lydia went in while Fancy was sleeping. She held the baby saying that she was beautiful. She looked at Fancy as though she was the father of the baby. She caressed her face as Fancy slept. I was watching from the corner and it hurt me that she showed that much emotion when it came to Fancy. I figured out she was sick soon enough when she started to plan a life for her, Fancy, and your daughter. I didn't hate Fancy; I felt bad for her because Lydia would kill her when she found out who Fancy was in love with. So I took my time getting close to Fancy not just to end her life, preciously, but also to protect her from Lydia. This obsession was growing even more and when she attacked her at the apartment, it was because Fancy refused to be touched by her. I just wanted to end Fancy's life smoothly because she could never live up to Lydia's expectations. You need to believe me. Lydia will not stop until Fancy accepts her."

Rich and Royce looked at Michael. They weren't sure what he was talking about.

"What are you talking about?" Royce asked. "She won't stop? Who else has she killed?"

Michael sighed. "There's about three more bodies out there that look like Fancy and she won't stop until the real one is with her. She wanted to come to the hospital that night when I almost ended Fancy's life. She was enraged that Fancy took your daughter and hid her. She felt as though she was betrayed so now to complete everything, Fancy must die."

Rich was officially angry. He was angry with himself for not figuring everything out ahead of time. He'd known this somehow had something to do with Fancy, but he could never put his finger on why.

He looked over at Michael who didn't see how sick he was too. He claimed that the serial killer, Lydia, was sick but he didn't take a look in the mirror to see his own reflection.

Rich looked at his partner then at Michael and said, "We're done here."

With that, Rich and Royce left the hospital room.

****

It was three in the morning when Rich got the call from Royce that they had the location Michael had given them of where Lydia was. Rich looked over at Fancy as she slept peacefully. She snuggled in closer to him as though she knew he had to leave. He traced over her eyebrows, her little nose, and her full lips on which he planted a soft peck. Fancy's eyes sprung open and she stared at Rich. Rich didn't want her to see the worry in his eyes, so he decided to distract her. Rich pulled her close to him again and she turned around to spoon with him.

Rich loved every part of Fancy's body after holding her tight. Rich knew Fancy loved cuddling.

Fancy couldn't sleep because she became restless so Rich made her relax. He started by kissing her neck, making her relax even more, and she cuddled closer to him. He nibbled on her ear, turned her around to face him, and kissed her forehead, her eyes, her nose, her cheeks, and then gave her a peck on the lips. Fancy stared at Rich, wondering if he really just gave her a peck. She reacted by kissing him, and she felt butterflies when he kissed her back.

She knew Rich didn't like someone else being in control so she smiled when he shifted and got on top of her. He took off her shirt and smiled at the fact that she didn't have anything on underneath. He started by kissing her neck, then he started a trail from her neck slowly going all the way down to her breasts, and he worshipped her perfect breasts with his tongue. He told her that her body was his and there wasn't a day or night when he didn't think about them. Fancy loved the way he was talking to her, like he'd read a book on how to please her. Then…Rich finally entered her.

He paused for a second.

"What's wrong baby?" Fancy asked.

Rich looked down at her and smiled. "Nothing. I just wanted to pause and feel you around me for a second. I don't ever want to forget how good it feels to be inside you."

Fancy smiled as Rich started to move.

He started out really slowly. Fancy opened up her legs wider for him, and he picked one up and pushed it towards her head. Fancy was feeling like she was on a different level because the way Rich rolled his hips slowly, sensually, making sure she felt every inch of him inside her. She couldn't forget him even if someone tried to make her. The way he was making her feel was pushing her pass her limits.

Rich never picked up the pace, not once, and she thought she would burst especially the way he was making sure she felt and heard everything—their breathing, the sweat dripping from their bodies, the way he drove inside of her. Fancy forgot how loud she could get until Rich picked up the pace a bit. It was as if he was following a rhythm in his head, kissing her and telling her to let go as he sucked on her ear. Fancy didn't realize she was on cloud nine until it was time for her to come back down to earth.

Rich collapsed on top of her and stayed there. After half an hour, he started to move. He looked at Fancy and she was fast asleep. He stood up slowly so that he could get ready to go meet Royce. He went in the bathroom, washed up, and came back in the room to get dressed. As he finished, he picked up his keys, his cell, and looked back at Fancy who was still sleeping. Rich sat back on the bed and leaned closer to Fancy. He saw the scrunched up face she made as she slept, the lines between her eyebrows. He made her relax as he massaged between her eyebrows with his thumb.

She relaxed her face, and he kissed her forehead before he got up to leave. He looked at Fancy sleeping and shook off the feeling of not seeing her again, especially dealing with this killer. He smiled at how beautiful she looked even when she slept.

Rich shook his head and walked out before he changed his mind and decided to just lie down in bed with Fancy, forgetting everything else.

"I love you," Rich said as he left.

Before he reached the door, he heard Fancy say, "Please don't leave, Rich."

Rich held on to the doorknob. He didn't want to leave, but he had to. This was his job. He had to stop this woman from killing others just to get to Fancy.

"Baby, I have to go and you know that," Rich said.

"Just…just come back to me in one piece, Rich," Fancy said quietly.

"I will, Fancy," Rich replied and walked out of the room.

Chapter 8

Rich felt the tightness of the ropes embedded into his skin as he pulled on them. He hated that he was tied to a chair and that it wasn't going to be as easy getting out of them as he thought. He figured he had to distract her as he tried to ease both his pain and the ropes.

Rich looked around the room he was in; the room definitely gave him the creeps. It was a disgusting and dirty abandoned clinic. He caught sight of a rat running from one area to the next and shuddered at the thought of how many rats were all over the place. He truly hated rats.

The place reminded him of an episode of a television show that showed the abandoned places all over the world. He wouldn't have been surprised this place had been on there.

The windows were still intact. All Rich could see were trees, and he wondered how long he had been out in order to be somewhere he didn't recognize. He shut his eyes temporarily, trying to muster up all the rational thoughts he had left before setting this psycho off, putting not only him, but also his love at risk.

He strained to remember and then it hit him: he'd left his parents' house and met Royce at the location. When he got there, he went outside to wait for his partner, but then something hit him in the back of his head. He knew that Lydia hadn't acted alone. It wasn't Michael either; there'd been someone else at play. Someone strong enough to pick him up and drag him to a different location. He figured it was a male because there was no way she could've dragged him, but as he tried to think about who else it could be, Lydia asked him a question.

"Oh so you're not going to talk?" The person asked him.

Rich heard footsteps coming closer to him. She finally appeared in his face and he was taken back. This person looked like a spitting image of Melissa. If it weren't for the blonde hair, he would've been fooled to think that it was Melissa. When she saw his reaction, she smiled. Rich looked at her something was wrong with her. She wasn't okay and he could see it in the way that she studied him, the curiosity in her eyes. Without any warning, she kissed him. He tried to move away but she held him there with her hands. When she finally let go, Rich spat on the ground.

"What's wrong with you?" he angrily asked.

"Nothing." She smiled. "I wanted to know what it is Francesca felt when she kissed you, but I see it's really nothing."

"Michael told me about your little fascination with my girl," Rich said as a matter of fact.

She started to laugh, the kind of laughter that gave Rich the chills, but he cleared his throat and continued. "Honestly Lydia, you think she'll leave me for you?"

Lydia stopped laughing and became serious. "How do you know my name?" she asked.

"That's your name? Or should I call you, Monica?" Rich asked.

Her demeanor changed; she looked at him with such hatred in her eyes. For Rich, that was what he wanted. He wanted to bring her to the point where she snapped so that he could control the situation.

Monica Whitfield had been Lydia's birth name, but when she turned old enough to change it, that was what she did. She felt disgusted every time the name came up. That name was a reminder that no one wanted her, she wasn't worthy of being loved, and that she lived in the shadows.

Lydia looked at Rich. This kind of information was hard to find. She had buried it really deep and no one but Michael knew. She shook her head; she knew what she had to do after. She had to get rid of Michael. Yes, she loved him like her own brother, but this was betrayal and betrayal didn't sit well with her.

Lydia took deep breaths to get rid of the dreadful feeling coming over her. It was time to concentrate and get rid of this annoying pest. She looked at Rich who was staring right back at her. He was like a thorn in her side. Lydia thought about how much he got in the way of everything, from trying to be with her sister to being around Fancy. Lydia came to the conclusion that it was Rich's fault that she'd had to end Melissa's life.

Lydia thought about how she would've changed her name back to Monica so that she could live freely. She'd dreamed of a life different from the one she was currently living, but there was one person who'd pulled that rug from under her…and this person was right here in front of her.

Rich Bautista, Rich Bautista, Rich Bautista. The name repeated in her head like a chant.

Rich looked at Lydia as she was making all sorts of faces and shaking her head at whatever she was thinking. He knew she was crazy, but being up front and center with it all made him sick.

Lydia abruptly stood up, knocking back the chair she was sitting on. She was pacing back and forth, talking to herself, trying to call herself down.

"Oh my, Oh my. I can't believe that this is about Rich. Really? Lydia calm down," Lydia said to herself. "Calm down, Lydia!" She yelled at herself again. She was getting irritated that she couldn't calm herself down.

She sat down on the ground and began rocking back and forth to calm herself down. Rich watched her from where he was sitting. He took this chance to get his feet a bit looser. Lydia continued talking to herself. "No one can take anything away from you. It's yours, you hear me? Do you hear me, Lydia? I'm talking to you."

Rich watched the interaction go on for a minute longer., He'd known she was sick, but this was a different level of sick. Then he watched her stand up and walked up near him. She grabbed a syringe that had some sort of liquid in it and emptied it into her arm. Lydia closed her eyes as the liquid ran through her body. It took her a second to react as she just stood there with her eyes shut.

"Finally," Lydia said with a breath of relief. "You know, she was getting on my nerves. All up in my head trying to tell me what I should or shouldn't do. She has no right. I let her stay, but she's trying to take over so I have to shut her up. Let me tell you something Rich, this girl is weak. I hate weak people and she just decides to be weak. I took her under my wing and protected her. I take in all the pain for her, I kill who I need to kill for her, and I endured every type of abuse that came my way but do you see the thanks she repays me with? She refuses to grow a backbone so I have to do everything.

"Let me tell you something. When I was taking care of Melissa, my twin, this girl decided to interfere and advise me to stop. She criticized me for not letting

Melissa live, but Melissa didn't deserve to live. I was doing the three of us a favor, if you ask me. Don't you look at me like that, Rich! You're looking at me the same way she does when I look in the mirror. None of you understand me. I'm tired of making people understand me. It's pointless, it really is!"

Rich didn't say anything; he wanted to understand her not to pity her, get why she was this way and how. It was something he was curious about.

It was silent for a minute and then Lydia continued. "The fact that this paranoid, good for nothing, feeling bad for people, trying to understand her own emotions heathen is in my head pisses me off. I need to permanently shut her up."

Rich looked at her as to why she'd said heathen. If she'd wanted to curse, she might as well have cursed instead of using a gentle word like heathen. So he spoke up and asked her.

"Heathen? I mean if you're going to curse, just curse honestly," Rich said, trying to sound annoyed.

Lydia looked at Rich and for a second, he saw how vulnerable she was.

"I don't curse," Lydia said with pride. "Growing up in the foster care system, we had a rule and that was no cursing. You see, I'm a Christian, so I can't curse."

Rich blinked rapidly as he tried to register what she'd just said. "What? You're a Christian? You do realize with Christianity, you're not supposed to kill? It literally says 'thou shalt not kill.' It's one of the Ten Commandments."

He was actually glad that he was forced to go to Sunday school as a kid.

Lydia just scoffed and shook her head. She didn't need anyone to teach her about the bible. She knew the bible from Genesis to Revelations. She could recite the bible, so she knew that what she interpreted had been the right thing. Her Sunday school teacher used to help her interpret the bible until one day he went as far as to touch her. Lydia said nothing when he'd roamed his dirty hands over her body, reciting a verse in Psalms. She would never forget the rage that came over her that day, which was the day she'd stepped in to take care of the other weak one. The weak one let him touch her all over even though she was just thirteen. She remembered the exact first and for a second, she started reciting it.

"The Lord is my shepherd, I lack nothing. He makes me lie down in green pastures, he leads me beside quiet waters, and he refreshes my soul. He guides me along the right paths for his name's sake. Even though I walk through the darkest valley, I will fear no evil, for you are with me; your rod and your staff, they comfort me. You prepare a table before me in the presence of my enemies. You anoint my head with oil; my cup overflows. Surely your goodness and love will follow me all the days of my life and I will dwell in the house of the Lord forever. Amen."

Lydia finished the prayer with a shudder. She remembered when she finished that prayer, he'd forced himself on her and told her not to tell a soul or she'd be kicked out. When everyone was sleeping, thirteen year-old Lydia had snuck into the Sunday school teacher's room with the kitchen knife that she stole. She didn't hesitate as she slit his throat; his blood splattered everywhere including her clothes and her face. That was the first time she tasted blood, when some got into her mouth. The killing had fascinated her as she'd watched the way he'd gasped for air, and as he took his last breath. That was the first time ever Lydia was content with her life. She knew that every life had a purpose as the Sunday school teacher had said so, and she knew that this was her purpose in life: to end the lives of those who felt they could do whatever and get away with it.

Rich watched Lydia as she licked her lips. He didn't understand her at all, but he knew something had happened to her with the way she drifted into no man's land. Lydia pulled the chair back closer to Rich as she stared at him.

"Lydia? I get that something happened to you," Rich said trying to get through to her. "I can see the look in your eyes but that doesn't mean what you're doing is right."

She switched up on her and shut the vulnerable one out. "You know nothing about me, Rich Bautista. You think you know because of poor little Michael? He doesn't know me either. None of you do. If you did, then I wouldn't be alone in this world."

Lydia looked down.

"First of all, you weren't alone in this world," Rich said angrily. "You had Michael but he wasn't enough for you. You had your twin, whom you killed."

"*I did it for you! She was cheating on you!*" Lydia yelled in Rich's face. Before Rich could get another word out, she punched Rich repeatedly until his face was full of blood. Lydia stopped and breathed loudly.

"She wasn't cheating on me," Rich said. "She was part of my team. She was a cop. You killed your innocent twin all because you were jealous of her. Don't use me as an excuse for your hatred, Lydia."

"You know nothing. All you're trying to do is confuse me so that I'll let you go, but know that I'm not letting you go. You're dying here like the rest of them," Lydia said.

Rich looked at her with no emotion. "I didn't plan on letting you go either. If I'm dying here, so are you pretty lady." He finished the sentence with a smirk.

"Shut up," Lydia said while she injected something into Rich.

Rich screamed as the substance ran through his veins. He felt like his whole body was being torn apart. He couldn't hold it in even if he tried. He screamed at the top of his lungs. Lydia started laughing. She loved that he screamed. It made her happy.

"I love that sound so much more than when you're talking," Lydia said.

Rich finally was able to breathe. His gray tee shirt was soaking in his sweat. *This isn't going to be how things end,* Rich thought to himself. He knew that his team would find him sooner or later due to the cell phone in his pocket. He knew that Lydia was in a rush because she didn't bother removing anything from him except for his gun.

Lydia dragged a chair in front of Rich and held his gun in her hands as she pointed it at him. "You took everything away from me Rich, you know that! You took my sister from me, you're trying to take my precious Francesca from me, and you took my baby away from me. You know Reese isn't yours, she's mine!" Lydia screamed.

Rich shook his head from side to side. He knew she was unraveling and it pleased him. "She's not yours, Lydia. I never took anything from you. You took my friend, Melissa, from the both of us. You chose to end her life just because of selfish reasons. Don't blame me for being sick in the head, do you hear me?" Rich yelled back at her.

"I'm sick?" Lydia asked.

Rich looked at her, filled with disgust. Then he felt a burn on his side as he realized that Lydia had shot him out of anger. He couldn't even reach for his side as he cried out in pain. He started to cough up blood, and wished that he were free and able to end her right there, right now!

Rich finally stopped coughing and looked at her with eyes full of rage. "You're dying by my hands."

Lydia laughed as she shot him again in the same area. Rich screamed louder than he had ever screamed in his life. Then she abruptly stood and injected him with the same substance, making him scream again. Tears came down his bloody face and she licked both the tears and blood, giving Rich goosebumps as he tried to move his face away from her tongue.

"You taste amazing, just as amazing as Francesca," Lydia said as she went back to sit in front of Rich. "If I didn't love her, I'd love you, but I choose her."

As Lydia had her back turned, Rich was able to get his legs loose. He used all his strength to lift himself up and use his legs to choke her. He refused to let go until he heard her voice straining. He knew she wasn't dead, but he waited until she was knocked unconscious. He tried his best to free himself using his teeth to get his wrists free.

It took him almost half an hour to get out of everything and when he did, Lydia was waking up. She tried to lunge at him and he leaped out of the chair. Lydia grabbed his leg and Rich fell on his wounded side. He screamed out in pain, but turned around to kick her in the face so she could let go of him.

Rich looked at where his gun had dropped when he was choking Lydia. He rushed over to get it and she hit him on his shoulder with a hammer. Rich was running on adrenaline so he didn't register the pain as he grabbed his gun, turned around, and emptied the rest of his bullets inside her. Lydia dropped right on him, bleeding out on him. She coughed and laughed at the same time. Rich felt her heartbeat above him as it slowed down until it didn't beat any longer.

As Rich felt his own life slip away, he smiled at the fact that his girl and his daughter would be okay now. He wasn't sure if he was losing it or what, but he could've sworn after however long it was, he'd heard his people coming in. By the time they found him, Rich was already unconscious.

****

It was now eleven at night and Fancy hadn't heard a word from either Rich or Royce. She wasn't sure what to do. She felt that something was wrong but what could she do? She hated what was going on and it made her uncomfortable.

Fancy was in the room trying to get her mind off of everything when she heard Mrs. Bautista scream. Fancy's heart started to beat so fast as she raced down the stairs to see what was going on.

"Mrs. Bautista! Mrs. Bautista!" Fancy screamed.

When she reached the living room, she saw cops. She stopped dead in her tracks as she saw Royce but no Rich. Royce started advancing towards her but she moved back, shaking her head from side to side.

"No! Royce No!" Fancy said.

"Fancy, please. I'm sorry," Royce said with regret in his eyes.

Fancy dropped to the floor and starting sobbing out loud. She couldn't contain it. She couldn't stop screaming and shaking. She was having a panic attack as she cried out for Rich. She knew what that sorry coming from Royce meant. It was the same sorry she'd received when Melissa was killed.

Rich's mother ran to Fancy and held her as she cried until she had no more tears to cry. Rich's mother rocked her back and forth, shushing her until she became quiet. The humming coming from Rich's mother soothed Fancy, but it didn't help the pain in her heart that she felt at the moment. She didn't know what to do or what she could do at the moment. Then Fancy thought about why Rich left in the first place, and she became angry.

"Mrs. Bautista? Did she die?" Fancy asked about the killer.

"Hush, baby," Mrs. Bautista said to her.

"No, tell me," Fancy insisted.

"She's dead," Mrs. Bautista reassured her.

Two days later, Fancy was still in a daze. She didn't know whether she would ever wake up not missing Rich or thinking about Rich.

Elisabeth

Chapter 9

~One year later~

Today made a whole year that Rich died. Fancy always wore his sweater or something of his as a good luck charm. She tried not to cry while on the plane back to California. There were so many memories of him that were rushing at her all at once. She missed everything about him: the way he laughed, the way he'd called her each morning to wake her up, his touch, his kisses,.even the stupid fights they had. Fancy had really tried to get herself together, but she couldn't.

She wiped her tears and told the stewardess to watch Reese for a minute while she used the bathroom. When she got into the bathroom, she put her hand over her mouth and cried hard. She didn't care if someone heard her crying. She missed Rich so much that she thought her heart would break at the way she cried. What made her want to sob even more was her last image of him, when he was going to find the killer, even though she'd asked him not to go. He'd kissed her goodbye and told her that he would be back, but he never came back. When they found him, he was gone and all alone. Rich was her soul mate and Fancy knew she would never be able to love anyone as much as she loved Rich. When he died, he took her heart with him and no one could ever retrieve it from wherever it was now.

She pulled out her phone and looked at pictures in her phone. She clicked on the one of her and Rich at the police fundraiser gala five years ago, the same night she got pregnant with Reese. She looked at his beautiful face as he smiled brightly. He looked handsome in that all black, Tom Ford suit.

Fancy shut her eyes and thought about his scent. He always smelled amazing. She smiled because she'd bought him Burberry cologne and ever since then, he'd stuck with that.

She swiped to the next one of Reese and Rich. He had her on his shoulders as Reese was laughing with her head thrown back a little. Fancy wiped a tear from her eye. She thought about how Rich wouldn't be there to watch Reese grow up and how Reese couldn't call her Daddy when she needed to. Fancy felt as though someone had stuck a knife into her heart and refused to remove it. The tightness she felt made her rub her chest. This hurt more than anything.

****

After a year, Fancy breathed the fresh air of California. She missed the busy things there. It was Reese's fifth birthday in a week, and she promised her paternal grandparents that she would bring her back to celebrate.

Fancy had returned to Ottawa when she'd lost Rich. Everything around her reminded her of him, so she took up the rest of her residency for psychiatry. The university of Ottawa gave her a job which she accepted with the advice of Rich's mother: *"Fancy, Baby, listen. I know how much my son loved you and there is no denying that. The way he looked at you was as if he'd never seen a more beautiful woman in his life. There were times where I would look at him as he looked at you. He looked at you as though no one else was there. There was nothing that would've stopped him from sacrificing everything for you and our little Reese. I raised my son right. I raised him to protect his family and that's what he did. I miss my Rich just as much as you, but we have to continue living not just for ourselves but also for our Reese. You hear, honey?"*

Her advice had stuck with Fancy when she'd felt like running back to California again, but had known she couldn't do it.

Fancy released another breath as she walked out of LAX with a sleeping Reese in one arm and their luggage in the other hand. As she was going down the escalator, she saw Mrs. Bautista there, patiently waiting. Mrs. Bautista smiled and waved, causing Fancy to chuckle a bit at the sight. She'd truly missed her even though seeing her brought back memories of Rich.

Fancy shook off the depressive state that she was about to sink into as she got closer to the bottom of the escalator. As soon as stepped off the escalator, Mrs. Bautista hugged her tightly with Fancy hearing her sniffles.

"Oh, my Fancy, I've missed you dearly and my baby Reese too. Thank you for agreeing to this. Now I have a surprise for both of you guys," she said.

Fancy smiled. "We missed you too. Much more than you know. I am very glad I did come back. Now if you would just please take your heavy granddaughter."

Fancy passed an undisturbed sleeping Reese to her grandmother.

Fancy followed Mrs. Bautista to the car. When she got closer, she had this uneasy feeling. She tried shaking it off, and felt as though maybe it was just the reminder of what happened here a year ago. She felt like she was being watched, then she turned around and her steps faltered.

Fancy turned around and met the same green eyes she hadn't seen in a year. Her steps faltered, leaving her paralyzed on the spot. She shook her head thinking that maybe she was seeing things. She wasn't sure what to do or say. Just then, Mrs. Bautista turned around to ask her what was taking so long.

"Fancy? Darling, what's taking you so long to come and walk towards the car?"

Then Mrs. Bautista's gaze followed to see what she was looking at. Mrs. Bautista sighed and felt guilt overwhelm her. She knew that Fancy would be surprised with who she was about to see but she'd wanted to tell her before all of this.

Mrs. Bautista hurriedly tried to explain herself to Fancy. "Fancy, wait. Before you jump to conclusions, hear me out?"

Fancy finally found the ability to move again and looked at Mrs. Bautista. Confusion, anger, and hurt were all mixed in as she displayed each one more than once. She couldn't find her voice to speak, so she just stared.

"Fancy, wait for me here. Don't move. I'll be right back," Mrs. Bautista said with a pleading look on her face.

Fancy watched as Mrs. Bautista walked over to Rich, or his doppelganger, and spoke to him briefly. Rich seemed to understand what she was saying and looked over at Fancy again. Fancy looked away. She didn't understand why he wouldn't have told her that he was alive. This hurt her and she tried not to break down and cry. All that she knew was that Rich had died and that this was just a corpse.

She shuddered at her crude way of dealing with this. She felt as though she'd died inside when he died. Rich took her heart with him when he passed away. She remembered how she didn't get to see his body for the last time. She thought about how she'd told him to come back to her yet he hadn't made it.

Elisabeth

When she looked back at Rich and his mother, she saw that he was now holding Reese in his arms. He was now walking towards her, and as he walked by her he kept staring at her but said nothing. Fancy didn't understand who this man was that he could just walk by her.

She turned around and grabbed him by the back of his shirt, pulling him back towards her. Fancy was livid. She wanted Rich to face her and tell her what the hell was going on. Nothing was okay to her so she needed a clear explanation right now or she would get on the plane back to Ottawa and never look back.

Through clenched teeth, Fancy spoke. "Rich, I want you to explain to me why you think it's okay to hold my child and walk past me like you don't know me? Explain it now or I swear to God on my every own soul, I will *kill* you with my bare hands."

As Fancy said her last words, she was past the point of angry. This level of anger shook her whole body. She felt a major headache coming but she refused to back down even as her hands visibly shook.

Rich turned around to look at this small human being that had just threatened him. When he'd first seen her exit the airport, she'd captivated him. Everything about her was beautiful. When they made eye contact, he wanted to drown in those big brown eyes filled with sadness and confusion. He didn't understand how, but there was a longing in those eyes, a longing he wished was meant for him. His mother told him that she was someone who could possibly trigger his memory, but so far he got nothing.

When his mother handed him the little girl, there was a familiarity in the way he held her. When he held her, he felt a longing he hadn't felt being around his family. He wanted to understand what it was about this little girl.

He snapped out of it when he realized this gorgeous woman named Fancy was still tugging at the back of his shirt. He turned around as much as he could since she refused to let go of his shirt. Rich finally spoke up. "Hello, my name is Rich and I'm assuming you're Fancy. Can you let go of my shirt so we can talk?"

Fancy looked at Rich as he spoke those words and she didn't seem to understand what was going on.

"What's wrong with you, Rich? Do you not know me or something?" she asked.

Rich felt a familiarity with her, the same as he felt about the little girl, but what he didn't understand was, how did he know them?

" I-uh- I'm sorry, but do I know you from somewhere?" Rich asked.

As soon as Rich asked that question, Fancy let go of all the emotions she was holding back. Tears flowed down her face. She just didn't understand. Was this a sick joke that someone was trying to play on her? Did no one understand how much she loved Rich that they would cruelly do this to her?

Rich didn't even think twice when he reached out to wipe away her tears. It felt so natural to him as he did it. He loved the feel of her skin against his fingertips. He loved the color of her skin. Everything about her, he seemed to love. Was this the person that his brother, Mason, was trying so hard to help him remember? He noticed the way she held her breath as he wiped her tears away. He saw the love in her eyes as she stared at him. He looked from her eyes to her lips, and something was urging him to kiss her but he felt like she might slap him. He hadn't realized that his fingers started touching her lips which were full and inviting. Inviting him to kiss her, to express whatever feeling he didn't know was brewing inside of him. To have her explain to him what it was that was between them with those lips. Rich also realized not once did she pull away from his touch, not once did she flinch at the way he touched her. She was too used to his touch and it seemed as though he was used to her touch, her body. Rich made a promise to himself that he had to try and remember. He had to remember who Fancy was and what she meant to him.

****

Fancy couldn't stop feeling Rich's fingertips on her even as they drove into the Bautista home. Fancy told herself that Mrs. Bautista had convinced her to come and understand what happened to Rich, but it was because of Rich himself that she came. During the whole ride back, Fancy and Rich kept looking at each other through the rearview mirror as he drove. Fancy felt like she was in a dream. She told herself that she needed to wake up so that she couldn't hurt her own heart again.

Mrs. Bautista was the first one to enter the house with Fancy holding a sleeping Reese and Rich bringing in the luggage. When they arrived, Mr. Bautista walked over and hugged Fancy. He had an apologetic look when he saw Rich come in right after. He mouthed, "I'm sorry" as Reese started to stir in her mother's arms. Fancy gave a weak smile and indicated that she had to put Reese to bed. She walked away and went up the stairs to Rich's old bedroom, setting Reese down to sleep.

Reese started to stir some more so she sat down rubbing her daughter's back and humming a melody. Reese finally fell back to sleep and Fancy watched her daughter. She didn't know what she was going to tell her when she woke up. How could she even begin to break her daughter's heart all over again if he didn't remember her? Reese loved her father just as much as he loved her, but he didn't remember.

Fancy sighed loudly. She turned and was ready to stand up then Mrs. Bautista came in.

"Fancy, let me explain everything," she said.

Mrs. Bautista started telling her about the phone call they'd received a couple of days after she left. She told Fancy that she hadn't wanted to alarm her without proof of what the FBI was saying. They were told that Rich had Post-Traumatic Amnesia; he didn't remember anything that happened before the accident

Mrs. Bautista explained to her why they hadn't contacted her and that she knew she should've done so, but his progress hadn't been getting any better. Mrs.

Bautista also told her that the FBI said he was a really great asset to have on their team because none of his policing skills were lost. Although his family was against the idea, Rich said he wanted to do it, to remember, to trigger something. Rich had awful untimely episodes and she hadn't wanted her or Reese around him until he got better. The only thing that seemed to keep him at bay was the work he did with the FBI. The more he worked, the less he was likely to have an episode.

Mrs. Bautista told her that she thought maybe it was time to let Fancy and Rich meet, and that Fancy could probably be the one to trigger the memories. After sitting there for a while silently listening to Mrs. Bautista, Fancy spoke up.

"Mrs. Bautista, I understand, I really understand where you are coming from. I would've done the same for Reese but the thing is, I wouldn't have kept it away from her for that long. A year, a whole year, I mourned him. I loved Rich with every inch of my body, every fiber of my being, and he was snatched away from me not once but twice. It hurt when he died. It felt like someone literally ripped my heart out. I couldn't properly eat, sleep, or do anything when I left, but I decided to do it because I had another extension of him. I had Reese to take care of, to love, to be there for her just as he would've been. I need time to process this. I need to figure out what I'm going to do. This hurts, it really hurts."

Fancy finished with a sob. She was tired of crying. It hurt her every time she thought of the moment the news was delivered to her and now this. Fancy walked away from the room and left Mrs. Bautista there alone, sniffling. Fancy's vision was blurry as she hurried through the familiar house. Even at this moment, her contacts did not help her properly see.

As she opened the door to the bathroom, she ran right into Rich's chest. At that moment, she didn't care about anything. She hugged him, feeling the familiarity around her. She simply cried, cried for her baby Reese, cried for her broken heart, cried for Rich. She cried that someone had taken him from her and returned him with the sickening joke of not remembering her. Not remembering the love that they shared, the love in his heart for her. She wanted him back and she made up her mind that if she couldn't have the old Rich back, she would go through the gates of hell to snatch him right back he belonged, which was by her side.

Rich hugged a sobbing Fancy back. At first he went rigid, unsure what to do or how to react to her, but it was as if he melted and instinctively put his arms around her.

Elisabeth

She felt so right in his arms, like she belonged there, so why was it that he couldn't remember? Did something happen to them? The doctor told him that he suffered injuries while working to stop a serial killer, but he remembered his mother, his father, and his brother. Why couldn't he remember her?

Chapter 10

In the last couple of weeks that Fancy was there, Rich's family knew they did the right thing by asking her to come back. Mrs. Bautista watched Rich as he played outside with Reese. He didn't fully remember her, but there were bits and pieces that came to him at random times. Rich's psychiatrist from the FBI told her that he would be able to gain his memory back soon enough and that his chaotic episodes had stopped. Rich's psychiatrist thanked Mrs. Bautista for bringing back the pieces to Rich's puzzle. Rich had made a lot of progress from being out on the fields to agreeing to get to know Fancy and his daughter all over again. Mrs. Bautista smiled as she looked at how Rich pretended to get hurt while Reese ran over to him to make sure he was okay. Fancy was busy preparing with Mrs. Bautista to get Reese's birthday party started.

Today was the day; it was Reese's fifth birthday. As the other parents came in with their kids that hopefully remembered her, Fancy was nervous for Reese. She wanted her baby girl to have a wonderful time, to be able to celebrate it and have her wishes come true. Tugging at her dress distracted Fancy, and she looked down to see Reese smiling up at her with her two front teeth missing.

"Hello, baby. What can I do for you, princess?" Fancy lovingly asked her daughter.

"Hmm, Mommy, can I have some candy?" Reese asked, still smiling up at her mother.

Fancy playfully gave her a stern look and shook her head. "No can do, Missy. You'll be having chocolate cake soon so you know what that means right?"

Reese nodded, agreeing with her mother.

"Yes, Mommy," Reese disappointingly said.

"Okay now, do you know what you're going to wish for?" Fancy asked her.

Reese got excited again and said, "It came true already."

"What did you wish for?" Fancy asked.

Reese pointed at Rich, who was entertaining the other kids, and said, "I wished for my Daddy to come back and he did."

Fancy stared at her baby girl and tried not to cry. She loved this girl and felt blessed to be her mother. She kissed the top of Reese's head before Reese ran back to get her father's attention.

****

At Reese's birthday dinner, everyone was having a great time talking and chitchatting. Rich kept looking at Fancy. He didn't fully remember yet, but everything about her made him happy. It was like the moment she stepped off that plane and locked eyes with him, he was forever lost in those eyes. This woman that he couldn't remember had given him the most precious gift—his daughter. Rich felt like Fancy was a selfless, amazing, gorgeous woman who had taken care of their daughter in his absence, and who'd loved him in his absence. She carried on his memories even though she thought he'd died. Rich felt such love and gratitude towards this woman. He didn't know how, but although she was ripped out of his memory, the love became stronger even without it. Rich knew that in that moment, he would protect her to his very last breath. He would cherish and love her if she allowed him. If his old memories never came back, he was willing to build new memories with her because she was his and he would forever be hers. No matter where they were, they would always make it to each other. She was his soul mate, his everything.

Rich looked at her. He looked at how beautiful she was from her form-fitting dress to her shoulder length hair. The bob shaped her oval face and her black-rimmed glasses made her even more attractive. He just wanted to kiss her, to feel her lips on his again. He missed everything about her, especially her kisses. He didn't even understand how he'd endured an entire year without calling her.

He watched her movements as she put one leg over the other. It hiked her dress up a bit, which made him smile. He saw that her leg was shaking so he looked up at her face. When he did, Fancy tilted her head to the side. He stared at her for a while then she gave him the most heart-warming smile. Just then, memories started to flood through him. Rich felt overwhelmed and abruptly stood, walking to the kitchen. He needed a moment. All these memories were giving him a headache. He held his head as it pained him. He didn't want to disturb anyone so he didn't utter a sound. He wasn't looking up but someone handed him a glass of water. When he opened his eyes, he saw the woman he'd forgotten...Fancy.

With worry written all over her face, Fancy asked, "Are you okay Rich?"

Rich looked at her and kissed her. It took Fancy a minute to register what was going on but when she did, she kissed Rich back. Hard. She had refused to kiss him this whole time because she wanted him to be comfortable with her and Reese, but now she couldn't think of anything else she could be doing. Rich pulled away first then kissed Fancy on the forehead. Fancy wanted to cry at how much Rich was acting like his old self. She tried to shake that thought off because it wasn't his fault he wasn't him anymore.

Rich smiled as he said, "Francesca, baby. I'm back."

Fancy just stared at Rich as though he had just slapped her. She had nothing to say. Rich knew his girl, so he gave her a minute to let it all sink in and then Fancy started to cry and hugged him tightly.

Through tears, Fancy said, "Oh Baby, I thought I lost you forever. Oh thank you, thank you, for coming back to me. Oh I love you, I love you."

"I love you too, Francesca. More than you'll ever know. Now let's go give our family and friends a heart attack," Rich said as he kissed her again and she smiled.

****

The minute Rich called his mother and told her his memory came back, Rich's mother screamed.

Mrs. Bautista ran to her baby boy and hugged him. She didn't care about how or why, she was just overjoyed that her baby boy was back. Rich's dad joined in on the hug and was happy that his son was able to remember everything. Rich handled everyone's reaction pretty well, but what made him tear up was his daughter running to him yelling, "Daddy, Daddy Daddy!"

Rich kneeled down and opened his arms as Reese ran into his arms.

"Ohh, Reese I missed you," Rich said as a tear fell from his eye.

"Daddy," Reese said.

Reese didn't have much to say. She was just happy that her dad remembered everything. She hugged her father and didn't let him go until she fell asleep in his arms.

Reese's birthday party came to an end and all of the guests left and only the family remained. Rich told everyone that he was going to put her down and come back, but half an hour went by and he still wasn't back downstairs.

"I'll be right back," Fancy said to Rich's parents. "I'm going to go check on Rich. Reese probably woke up again and made a fuss about going to bed."

Fancy made her way upstairs. When she walked in, she fell in love all over again. There her man was, asleep on the bed with their daughter lying on top of him. Fancy smiled because Reese looked tiny in her father's arms. Fancy covered them with a blanket and was walking out when Rich said, "Francesca, I promised you that I would come back and here I am."

Fancy turned around and looked at Rich who smiled at her as he fell back to sleep.

****

This was the first month since Rich remembered, but Fancy was still having nightmares of Rich not being there anymore. Fancy woke up sweating because of the nightmare she had. She dreamt that Rich was still dead and this whole month wasn't real. She was breathing heavy as she wrestled out of her bed sheets. As she tried to do that, she fell off the bed. The minute Fancy fell off the bed, Rich came back from the bathroom. He saw that she was fumbling out of the sheets while on the floor and he couldn't help but laugh. Fancy looked over at Rich as he was laughing at the doorway not even helping her up. Fancy stood, looking at Rich up and down contemplating if she should reach for a pillow and throw it at him.

"It's not funny, Rich," she said as she picked up the duvet from the floor. She heard a groan from Rich as she bent over to do it. Fancy heard Rich's footsteps as he got closer.

"Hmm Fancy, I missed you so much you have no idea," Rich said as Fancy stood up and turned around to face him.

Fancysmiled as she said,"I'm sure you missed me after I told you I didn't feel it was safe to be an FBI agent, but you refused to listen to me."

Fancy rolled her eyes at Rich as he just stood there. Fancy had been terrified something would happen to Rich and she would never see him again. That he would actually turn up dead. She understood that he was good at his job, but this was too much for her to deal with. Then there was also what he refused to tell her about his job.

Fancycontinued on,"So you're not going to tell me why you won't quit that or what it is you do so we can at least know you're safe? It's what,top secret or something stupid like that?" Fancy stood there waiting for Rich to speak. He just stared back at Fancy. As much as Richwanted to tell her, he just couldn't.

"I know," Rich said, motioning for Fancy to take a seat on the bed as he knelt in front of her. "Listen babe, yes I said I wasn't going to be a detective anymore,but the FBI recruited me for one of their special teams that they've put together. I passed all of their tests; aptitude, physical, psychological. Although, I didn't remember it seemed that I was one of the best agents that they recruited. I know that you wanted to know why they would pick someone who had amnesia but they invested and trusted in my abilities. I'll tell you what I can because I don't want you thinking I abandoned my family or responsibilities."

Rich continued. "As my mom told you before, the FBi recruited five of us to be in their special team force. What we do,I can't tell you, but basically we take people like Lydia off the streets. The crime level here has really risen especially with people that aren't mentally well or are unstable. No, I can't tell you what exactly we do or how we go about doing it,but just know that I'm here trying to make the world a safer place for Reese. I don't do anything without thinking of her safety first or in her best interest, all right? Just trust and believe me when I say there was no way I stayed away from you on purpose. I missed your voice, God I missed the way you laughed."

Fancy understood where he was coming from,but she still needed him to know that she wasn't happy with it all. She didn't have a problem with him deciding to do

that kind of work because she knew that's all he'd want
to do and he wouldn't sit still.

"Listen Rich, I understand it all and your reasons
for doing this, but give me some time to get over being
upset about you not leaving the job. What you do may
have been for the good of our daughter,but that doesn't
mean it doesn't hurt. I'm actually kind of relieved that
you chose to not fully give up on what you love. I know
how much you love this kind of work, and I wouldn't
take you away from it because I know you wouldn't take
me away from what I love."

Rich smiled and decided to not fight her on getting
over it so quick. He kissed her on the forehead. Fancy
closed her eyes. She was happy that her love Rich was
still alive and nothing was wrong with him anymore. As
Rich stood up, Fancy looked at where Lydia had shot
Richand she couldn't help but reach out and touch his

side. Fancy tried to shake it off,but she couldn't. She finally let it all sink in—how he 'd gone through everything, how he was tortured but was still able to return, to make it to her. Rich saw that Fancy was getting emotional and he kneeled back down to wrap her in his arms.

When Richwrapped his arms around Fancy, she let it all out. She started crying out loud and couldn't stop. These weren't tears of loss, they were full of thanks that he was alive, and there would be no more lonely nights without him, missing him. Rich just rubbed her back as she cried. He stood up and carried her, putting her back on the bed. When she was comfortably in the bed, Rich got in next to her and kept her close to him with her head rested on his chest.

Chapter 11

Fancy smiled as she stepped foot back in Rich's parents' home. She got a text from Rich telling her to meet him there. As she walked in through the front door, she looked on the floor. There were red and white rose petals trailing on the floor that Fancy followed. Fancy opened the patio door and gasped at the breathtaking scenery. Fancy looked over at her beautiful, handsome man standing there looking more than delicious. He standing near a candlelit dinner on the table took her breath away.

Fancy took in the rest of the patio's scenery. There was a passage way lit with beautiful candles leading Fancy to the table. Candles, both red and white, surrounded everything. As she got closer, Fancy took in

Rich's outfit. She loved it when he dressed casual, but he looked stunning in his all black dress shirt and black tie completed with black dress pants.

She drank him all in, unsure what to do. The questions that she had in her head all disappeared as Rich was talking. When he was talking, she realized that he was alive and well. She inspected him from head to toe; he was still the same handsome man that she fell in love with. His dark hair was cut short but he had much more facial hair than before. Fancy liked the facial hair. It made Rich look a bit rugged and she liked it. She wasn't sure what to do next but she couldn't help as she reached out to touch his hand.

Fancy wanted to feel Rich's skin as she caressed his big hands. Rich looked at Fancy as she did this small gesture, and he quickly wiped her tears away and kissed her. He didn't bother wasting anytime. He wasn't going to wait for her permission as he kissed her deeper. Rich broke the kiss and kissed Fancy on the forehead.

"I love you," he said to her.

"I love you too, Rich," Fancy replied.

"I know you do that's why I love you even more," Rich said to her.

Fancy chuckled a bit as she said, "This is so beautiful. Did you really come up with all of this?"

She looked around again.

"Yes baby, now come here." Rich pulled her closer, closing the gap between them.

Before Fancy could even answer, he was kissing her again. Even after all this time, kissing him was something that expressed more than enough. She still felt butterflies every time he held her hand, kissed her on her forehead, kissed both her cheeks but at this very moment, she was seeing stars.

What the heck? Fancy thought.

Rich finally stopped kissing Fancy. "Finally, babe," Fancy said with a smile.

Rich couldn't help but laugh at her. "Francesca, I did tell you that I missed you. Now sit." Rich gestured for her to take a seat.

Fancy took her seat and said, "I missed you too, baby."

All kinds of thoughts were running through Rich's mind as they sat throughout dinner. He had never been nervous about anything else in his life, but he was about to propose to this woman and that made him nervous.

He made sure she couldn't tell as he engaged her in silly conversations about everything, but as dessert came by, his nervousness kicked up a notch. As the dessert was being served, Fancy excused herself to the bathroom. She tried to hold it throughout the dinner, but she felt as though she would explode. After she finished, she walked back out thinking of what her and Rich could do for the weekend with Reese. As she stepped outside to the patio, she started to talk.

" Rich! You know what we could do this week—oh my God."

All she saw was Rich on one knee, holding out the most beautiful ring she'd ever since. *Jesus, that's some serious bling*, Fancy thought. It was a princess cut three-diamond Harry Winston ring. It was Fancy's favorite ring and she was going to cry.

Then Rich started talking. "Francesca Imani, I want to spend the rest of my life with you. I want you to be here when I wake up, when I go to sleep. I want you to be the one that fixes my lunch, makes my dinner. I want to spend the rest of my life cherishing you, taking care of you and our baby, babies to come." He smiled. "I want you to have more of my kids, be the mother of all my kids. I want to love you, fight with you. I want you to be mad at me, happy with me. I don't want to see you smile because of anyone else but me. I want everyone in this world to see who makes me angry, who makes me happy. I want you to be my wife, my best friend, my heart, and my all. Will you make me the happiest man alive and marry me?"

Rich slipped the ring on as Fancy started to tear up.

Fancy finally found her voice and said, "Yes Rich Bautista, I will make you the happiest man alive and marry you."

Just then Rich's parents and his brother finally appeared. "Oh my God...yes! finally!" Mason said.

Fancy turned around and saw all three of them with Reese in her grandfather's arms. Fancy smiled and asked Mason, "Mason? Where the heck did you come from?"

Mason pointed at the couch that wasn't fully in sight as he said, "We were hiding back there, Mrs. Bautista."

Fancy smiled because now she couldn't deny it because she was soon to be Mrs. Bautista.

"Stop it," Fancy said. She was feeling shy all of a sudden when Mason said that.

Mrs. Bautista walked over to Fancy and admired the ring. "God, I love you. Come here and give me a hug. I can't believe this day finally came. Fancy, thank you for saying yes."

Mrs. Bautista knew her son would be happy with Fancy because that was who he belonged with.

Fancy hugged Mrs. Bautista tight as she said, "Oh Mrs. Bautista, Mom, I love you too. Thank you for everything. Mr. Bautista, oh sorry I meant to call you, Dad. Thank you."

"No problem, Fancy. You've made me a proud grandfather and now a happy father-in-law. Love you honey."

Rich smiled at his parents. He held Fancy's face in his hands as he said, "Francesca, babe. I love you."

Without skipping a beat, Fancy said, "I love you too Rich." She smiled at him because she knew she would never get tired of hearing him say that to her for as long as she was alive. "I have to go call my Mom. She will be so happy." Fancy said without realizing how huge of a smile she had on her face.

Chapter 12

Fancy stared at herself in the mirror. she was wearing a traditional, beautiful white gown. It was a strapless ball gown, and the top half was sprinkled with diamonds.Fancy never thought that she would get a chance to wear a wedding dress made of diamonds. The puffiness of the ball gown made her feel like a princess and she loved the way it flowed, the way it made her feel.

The top half hugged her breasts and her waist, and she felt perfect. Then she looked at her face and didn't recognize herself. She looked so beautiful.

She started to cry as she saw her parents and Rich's parents come into the room. She looked over at her baby girl who was holding onto her Fancy's mother's hand.

Fancy smiled as she opened up her arms and her daughter ran into her them.

She picked up her daughter and kissed her on the forehead.

"I love you my Reese's pieces," Fancy said with a smile.

Reese smiled back at her mother, kissing her on the lips. Then Rich's mother walked towards Fancy and smiled at her. She cupped Fancy's cheek.

"I just want to thank you for walking into my son's life, Francesca. You are the best thing to ever happen to him and us. Thank you for little *Reesy* here. I love you."

She stared at Fancy and was at a loss for words. There was nothing that she could say because anything she thought of saying went out of her head. She thought that her son was the luckiest man alive to have such a beautiful bride to call his.

"Oh Honey, why are you crying?" Rich's mother asked.

Fancy wiped the tears from her eyes."I just want to say thank you. Thank you for having your precious son, for giving him an example of what love is and for letting him show that to me. I love you and my future father-in-law for gifting me this wedding. This is something any woman would ask for and I thank you for supporting Reese and I when Richwas gone. You mean the world to us."

As Fancy finished up, she hugged her future mother in law.

"Oh,my baby."Fancy's mother walked over to her to hug the two that were already standing there hugging.

Reese made a sound."Mommy, you're squishing me," she complained.

All three women laughed as they wiped away each other's tears.

The men looked over at each other, and smiled because they both had the same thought in their head…"Women."

Fancy's dad walked over to her, cleared his throat, and extended his elbow to his one and only daughter. "Shall we go?" he asked her.

Fancy smiled brightly at her father and said with confidence, "Yes, Daddy."

Rich was nervous for some reason. He didn't get why he was so damn nervous. It wasn't like he didn't know what his bride looked like. As he heard the song, *A Thousand Years,* start to play, he knew it was time to welcome his bride. This version reminded him of The

Piano Guys' version of Christina Perri's song, and he watched as Fancy's father proudly came in with his daughter.

Fancy looked far more beautiful than he'd ever seen. She was the most beautiful looking woman and to him, she looked like an angel in that beautiful white gown. She was smiling, but he knew that she was just as nervous as he was.

Fancy finally got to where Rich was standing and everything went by in a blur for the both of them, from the wedding vows to the kissing of the bride.

Fancy watched Rich having a great time sitting and chatting with his friends. She made a quick bathroom break since the alcohol was really starting to hit. It was such a process, especially with her wedding dress on. Rich's parents refused to wait more than two months since they conveniently had everything set for the wedding. Fancy agreed because she didn't know where to begin or end.

Fancy walked back into the hall as her song, *Somebody,* by Natalie La Rose and Jeremiah started to blast through the speakers. While in that big wedding dress, she started to dance by herself, then Rich's uncle, James, pulled her closer into the group of men he was with and started to dance with her. Rich watched as Fancy started to dance, and he walked over to grab Fancy because everyone knew Uncle James got a little too touchy when he was drinking. Fancy gave her wine glass to one of the servers and smiled at Rich as he pulled her closer to dance.

Fancy felt this weird, tingly feeling when Rich held her close. She didn't know what to say or what to do, but all she knew was that she loved feeling like this even until now. She smiled and closed her eyes, then Rich kissed her neck, sending shivers up her spine.

"Liked Uncle James did you?" Rich teasingly asked her.

Fancy smiled and shrugged her shoulders. "He seemed nice."

"Yeah, I'm sure he seemed like it. You're lucky he hadn't started to grope you or else you wouldn't think he's so nice."

Rich chuckled at the memory of many females slapping his uncle at any events they had when he was younger. All Fancy could do was laugh. What he didn't know was that if Uncle James had tried that, she should've punched him straight up.

A little while later, Fancy went to change and came back in wearing a Vera Wang mermaid wedding dress. It was strapless with diamond details under her bust, and it emphasized her curvy shape. The dress was made for Fancy as it hugged her shapely hips and then became puffy right above the knees. Royce tapped Rich to turn around and look at his beautiful bride who was coming in with champagne in one hand, and moving her hips to the song, *Hold My Hand,* by Jess Glynne.

When he turned, his heart skipped a beat. Fancy was beautiful beyond imagination. She was smiling at his mother as they came back in together, and she couldn't help but move her hips to the song. He knew that she was definitely tipsy and loosened up. He felt like the luckiest man alive when his other close and work friends complimented him on how beautiful she was and her body. He knew that he should keep his cool, but he felt himself getting angry every time his friends or anyone mentioned her body. As if she sensed him getting pissed off, Fancy made her way to him while still dancing. When she reached the table where he was sitting, she stood right in between his legs since he had them wide open.

Fancy stepped in even closer to him and said, "Hey husband."

Rich instantly smiled. "Hey wife," he responded trying to keep his cool.

Fancy drank her champagne and held her hand out for him to get up as she waited for him. She simply told him, "Come dance with me."

Fancy took his hand as she led him to the dance floor. Everyone seemed to sit down as if they were having a second, first dance. When the band started to play the song, *Last Time,* by Eric Benet, Fancy offered Rich the rest of her champagne and he drank it all in one big gulp. He gave it to the waiter that came around, then he took her hands and slowly brought them up around his neck. He didn't miss the slow breath intake she did when he ran her hands by his chest as he was bringing her arms up. His hands slowly felt her curves as they drifted down and stopped at her waist. Rich noticed the goosebumps on Fancy's arms and he bent down, kissing her shoulder.

Fancy was glad she wore heels that gave her a bit of a boost when it came to putting her arms around Rich's neck, even though he basically had to crouch down a lot more than she had to raise her arms. She noticed the look in his eyes when he kissed her shoulder. She thought that he was going to kiss her, but he didn't.

Fancy thought back to the first time she met this man. She didn't see them coming this far but here they were. They had a beautiful baby girl together, they loved each other, and they were married to each other. Fancy looked up at Rich. She had never wanted someone to kiss her so much, especially with the emphasis of the Eric Benet song. It did things to her because she wanted what he was describing in the song, and the way the guy was covering the song made her want to tear up. She was never sure she would've ever gotten this kind of love—a love that consumed you, a love that made you feel protected, a love that you would do anything for. Something that made you cry just because you knew how good you had it. When you kissed each other, you couldn't let each other go because it would make you feel incomplete. When they walked in a room, even with your back turned, you could feel them because your body only reacted to their presence. And, when you told them you loved them, you didn't feel like you were telling them enough so you continuously told them hoping that they would be the last person that you would love and spend the rest of your life with.

Rich saw that Fancy was so involved in the song she had so many different displays of emotions on her face.

He wanted to kiss them all away. Then the band started to play another song, *So Amazing* by Luther Vandross, and for some reason, he felt like some of the lyrics were speaking to him. He made Fancy face him and he tilted her chin up. He looked into her eyes and she stared back at his. He felt like she was seeing right through him. Yes, they were both tipsy so maybe that was the weird feeling in the air wrapping them up sort of like a cocoon that brought them closer to each other.

Fancy smiled at Rich. That smile captured his heart and he knew he would definitely be lost in her love forever with no regrets.

He bent closer to her face and kissed her. At first it was soft kisses just to see if Fancy would react and when she did, Rich deepened the kiss, not caring if anyone else was looking. He cupped her face with one hand and his other arm came around her waist, picking her up to his full length. Fancy couldn't really do much but put her arms around his neck. She wanted to feel him closer.

Rich broke the kiss first. He smiled at her, the biggest boyish smile she'd ever seen him sport. He looked so damned cute she didn't know what to do but just give him a peck before he set her back down on her feet.

They finally snapped out of it when they realized that everyone was clapping and cheering. Fancy was officially embarrassed. She wasn't one for too much public displays but for this man, she would claim him in front of everyone. There was nothing or nowhere else Rich or Fancy would rather be. This moment for them was going to be cherished forever despite the hardship they had to endure or the roads they had to travel. They were able to travel it together.

Rich looked into Fancy's eyes and kissed her again. He smiled because he'd fulfilled is promise to her. From the beginning, he'd told her that he was going to make her his wife, make her Mrs. Bautista, and that was what he did. Despite anything and everything, they made it to each other.

The End

CPSIA information can be obtained
at www.ICGtesting.com
Printed in the USA
LVOW01s2314050816
499271LV00018B/902/P